The Wolf's Mate Book 5: Bo & Reika

R. E. Butler

Copyright 2013 R. E. Butler
All rights reserved.

ISBN: 1497385334
ISBN 13: 9781497385337

Dedication

For Jacq McNeill, whose friendship means the world to me.
And to my fans and friends... thank you for your support.

Table of Contents

Chapter One	1
Chapter Two	12
Chapter Three	25
Chapter Four	34
Chapter Five	48
Chapter Six	58
Chapter Seven	65
Chapter Eight	73
Chapter Nine	79
Chapter Ten	87
Chapter Eleven	98
Chapter Twelve	105
Chapter Thirteen	116
Chapter Fourteen	126
About the Author	135

Acknowledgements

Cover Artist: Ramona Lockwood
Jennifer Moorman, Editor

Chapter One

Reika plopped down on the couch next to her younger brother, Ben, and peered over his shoulder. He was glued to the eBook reader, a digital cookbook page displaying a vivid picture of a bubbling dish on the screen before him. He loved to cook and had taken culinary classes at Columbus State Community College. Ben worked at a greasy-spoon as a cook, but one day he wanted to work in an upscale restaurant. For now, he was also the family cook, which their mother was thrilled with.

"What's on the menu tonight?" Reika ruffled his short black hair.

He patted down his hair with a scowl and then tipped the reader so she had a better view. "Spinach and ricotta manicotti."

She looked at the dish, a cheesy, gooey masterpiece of pasta and sauce. It looked delicious.

"Cool. Can you make me a peach smoothie for dessert? You know I love them." She grinned at him and stood.

"Isn't it a little cold for icy drinks?" He looked out the window towards the snow that blanketed the yard. They lived in a suburb of Columbus, Ohio that had seen more than its fair share of snow this past January.

"Never too cold for peach smoothies, Bro."

"They'll have to be canned peaches, Sis." His upper lip curled in disgust. To Ben, using anything except fresh produce was a culinary sin. Reika didn't care. He was a master in the kitchen and could make even canned peaches taste amazing.

"You'll make some woman a really great wife someday."

"Oh, ha ha, Kiki."

She enjoyed teasing Ben. Although they argued from time to time, they had a loving relationship. He was sweet, funny, and protective, even though Reika was almost three years older.

"Hey, I'm making your cake for tomorrow. What kind do you want?" he called to her as she walked towards the stairs.

Her steps faltered and she froze, her hand tightening on the pale oak banister. Her twenty-third birthday was tomorrow. *Maybe they'll forget about me*, she thought.

"Chocolate."

"You got it," he answered lightly.

She knew Ben also remembered that Saturday wasn't *just* her birthday, but he didn't say anything more, and she was relieved. The less she thought about the noose that tightened around her neck, the better.

Her footsteps felt suddenly heavy as she made her way up the stairs to her bedroom. She had spent her whole life in this home. She loved everything about it—the vanilla candles her mother liked to burn, the scent lingering in the air long after they had been snuffed; the height marks climbing the wall in the pantry, marking Ben and her as they grew; and the bay window in her bedroom with the specially made pillow her grandmother crafted before the arthritis stole her abilities.

She pulled her sweater tighter around herself as she hugged her arms around her middle and sat down, pressing her forehead against the cold glass of the bay window.

Sixteen years had passed since *the incident*. Even though she had a fleeting thought that they might have moved on, she knew in reality they wouldn't have changed their minds. Were-lynxes didn't forget their debts.

Were-lynxes were the gypsies of the were-world. The Cullaga lynx clan had traveled through Central Ohio when she was seven and took over the wooded area surrounding Buckeye Lake. Reika's wolf pack had been there for the Fourth of July, celebrating with a cookout, swimming, and boating. Reika's alpha, Grim, had warned their people to stay clear of the lynxes, but little Ben had been only four and fascinated with the horses tied up around their camp.

He'd unintentionally opened the makeshift gate of the horse pen, and the king lynx's prized Arabian had been injured when it escaped and had to be put down. Ben had been terrified. Hell, they all had been. Reika remembered when the lynx king brought Ben back to the area where the pack was enjoying the picnic, and Ben was white with fear. His small body trembled, and tears spilled down his cheeks. The king, Maurice, demanded payment for his horse—a horse he said was worth one hundred thousand dollars.

Reika's family wasn't poor, but they didn't have a lot of cash laying around. She'd stood behind her mother, fearful for her brother, wishing she were old enough to shift into her wolf-self so she could rip off the rotten old king's arm for touching Ben and making him cry.

The king suddenly noticed her as she peeked around her mother's body. He lifted his head, closed his eyes, and opened his mouth, scenting deeply, making a strange, rasping noise that caused shivers to race down her spine. Her mouth went dry, her heart pounded in fear, and her knuckles turned white as she clutched her mother.

"You," he said, pointing at Reika as she cowered behind her mom. "You are a qualfo, *a healer wolf." Looking at Alpha Grim, the king said, "We will take her. She will mate with my grandsons and produce a new generation of lynx-wolf healers."*

Reika didn't entirely understand all that he said, but she knew that mate *meant husband and wife and that her mother suddenly drew her into her arms and held her close enough that Reika could feel her shaking. The woman who had never been afraid of anything, now trembled in fear.*

"No," her mother hissed as her father came to stand with them. A growl seeped from his lips.

Alpha Grim snarled, "We do not give our children to become breeders. We will get you the money for your horse. Release the child, and be on your way."

"You will give us the girl, or we will kill the boy."

A young man, not more than twelve or thirteen, stepped forward and pulled a knife from his belt, pressing it against Ben's throat. A line of blood trickled down Ben's throat, and he whimpered.

The young lynx kept his eyes on Reika but said to Ben, "Hold still, little dog, or I might accidentally slit your throat before your pretty sister's eyes."

Ben then went very still, but his eyes widened and he bit down on his bottom lip, squeezing his little hands into fists as his body went rigid. Reika sobbed, burying her face in her mother's shirt.

Reika's father stepped forward. "We can work out an arrangement. I do not want to see our people come to blows over a simple accident."

The king sneered. "Our people number two hundred."

Reika knew what that meant. Their pack had less than sixty members. If the lynxes went to war with their pack, the wolves would lose. She could lose not only her brother, but also her parents and possibly her own life.

She tugged on her mom's arm. She looked down at Reika. "I'll go, Mama. I can't let them kill Ben."

Her mother dropped to her knees and hugged Reika tightly, sobs wracking her mother's body. A shadow loomed over them, and when Reika opened her eyes, she saw her father's face pulled taut with anger. "We'll make sure they won't come back for you until you're an adult, honey. That will give us enough time to find a way out of this."

"I know, Daddy." Reika believed him. Her father had never lied to her, prizing honesty above all else. If he said they'd figure out how to free her from the lynxes, then she knew he would. Somehow.

She stood between her father and Alpha Grim, with her mother right behind her. The king lynx stood with three young men, including the one who held the blade to Ben's throat, and the king introduced them as Josef, Eli, and Adam, his grandsons. They were tall and skinny, each with dirty blond hair that hung, matted, past their shoulders. Their clothing was worn and patched, and their fingernails looked like dirty half moons. The young men stared at her in a way that made her skin crawl. She wanted to run home and hide in her closet among the stuffed animals and dolls, but she had to be strong for her family and her pack. Her father said they'd figure it out, and his promise gave her strength to stand tall.

Alpha Grim and King Maurice talked with her father for a long time. The three boys never stopped leering at her, leaving her feeling nauseous and dirty. The summer before, she and her family had gone to a wildlife park and a giraffe had stuck its head in the window of the jeep they were in and licked the side of her face with its enormous, blue tongue. She thought that was the worst thing ever. But this—the way the young lynxes looked at her—was like getting licked by a hundred giraffes.

King Maurice wanted to take her when she turned sixteen, after she was able to shift for the first time, but her father and Alpha Grim angrily opposed that. Her father argued to let her have time to live her life and go to college, and finally, the lynx king agreed that she would be allowed to remain with her family until she turned twenty-three.

"Then it's decided," Maurice said finally. "The she-wolf healer will remain with her family and home pack until the sun sets on her twenty-third birthday. She will join our clan, willingly, and mate my grandsons and produce heirs."

When Maurice released Ben, he ran right to Reika, and she hugged him tightly. As the lynx clan turned and sauntered away, the oldest, Eli, looked at Reika and said with a cold voice, "We'll be seeing you ... wife."

Even now, sixteen years later, she got chills when she remembered the looks in their eyes—as if she was property, something to be used and passed around, and not a person. She was an *apex*, a she-wolf healer. She had come into her healing abilities at the age of sixteen when she shifted into her blue-black wolf form. All the women in her family were healers. In their wolf forms, their mouths secreted venom that could heal even the most severe injuries. They were prized as mates. The male who took an apex as a mate was lucky indeed.

But not the lynxes. They wouldn't think they were lucky; they thought they were entitled to her. To use her body, breed her, force her. She had no illusions about her future with them. Her life with the lynx clan would be violent and bloody, like a waking nightmare she would have no hope of escaping.

Her cell beeped, signaling a text message. She opened it, delighted to finally have a solution to her problem.

From WAA: Saturday at 5 a.m., two guards will meet you at LSV AA Terminal; bring one bag only. They will wait no more than thirty minutes before they will leave without you. Tell no one.

Her heart pounded in her ears, and she closed her eyes as relief rushed over her. The Were-Animal Alliance, a secret underground group that helped wolves like herself out of impossible situations, would give her a new identity and relocate her to a safe pack far away from her troubles. She had never heard of them until she was in a camping store with her father last month. She'd left him to look over tents and had wandered over to a community bulletin board. Some of the notices were very old, pinned beneath other, newer papers. She rifled through the pages and cards, seeing notices for spring festivals, pets lost or found, community-wide garage sales from the previous summer, and then, buried under several advertisements for a local bar, one page caught her eye. Simple black text emblazoned the white page: *Need Help? Text the Were-Animal Alliance.*

Her heart stopped for a moment as she read the two sentences a dozen times. Help? What kind of help? Could they help her? Her father called her name. She jerked the page from the bulletin board and stuffed it into her front pocket, joining her father at the register. Hope bloomed inside her like a hidden ember in a long dead fire. There was a group out there that *might* be able to help her. She hadn't felt hope in this way since her father had promised her all those years ago that he would figure out how to get her free of the promise to join with the lynxes. The page felt heavy in her pocket, as fear began to seep into her, twining with the hope and choking it like weeds on a flower. What if the WAA couldn't, or wouldn't, help her? Her heart raced as hope and fear battled together inside her, but hope won out. If the WAA was unable to help her, then she would run on her own.

Reika sent them a message immediately, terrified that her time was running short, and she would be forced to go with the lynxes. The WAA had contacted her through text messages after agreeing to take on her case. They promised to help her escape the situation and hide her. She had been waiting for final instructions and had worried, with her birthday so close, that she was not going to be able to escape.

Her parents had been desperate to find a way to break the promise to the lynx king, but she was bound to them in a blood-debt. The king had taken a drop of her blood and mixed it with drops from his grandsons, sealing the debt like a sacred vow. She could sometimes still feel the puncture of his claw in her fingertip. According to the lynx laws, the only way she could break the promise to the lynx males was if she found her truemate. By their laws, her truemate would have the right to fight for her, and only when he was victorious could he declare that she was his alone.

But she knew all about the lynxes. They were cunning fighters, ruthless when it came to possessing what they felt was owed to them. While her truemate was only one person, all three of the lynx males would fight him at the same time. A wolf could beat one lynx, possibly two. But not all three.

Even if she had found her truemate by now, she wouldn't have put him through that. She wasn't so selfish that she would find the one male meant to be hers just to send him to his death. She hadn't ever actively looked for her truemate for that very reason. Unlike other she-wolves her age, she hadn't gone to pack gatherings, bars where unmated males were known to hang out, or tried any of the shifter dating sites, hoping to find the one wolf who was perfect for her. And now...she was going to run. The WAA promised her a new identity, safety, and anonymity within a new pack.

The people who ran the WAA worked in anonymity, so she had no idea who they were or where they lived. The last few weeks had been stressful as she explicitly followed their instructions, which explained how she would escape without being found.

That night, as her family was finishing dinner, there was a knock at the door. No one moved for several moments, until a second and then a third knock kicked her dad into motion.

"No, Dad, I should answer. It's my responsibility," Reika said, pushing her chair away from the table and standing. She took a moment to tug on the cuffs of her sweater to give her suddenly trembling hands a moment to settle, but they only trembled more. As she walked to the door, she wondered if the lynxes were going to post guards around the home to make sure she didn't leave, and the unexpected thought made her blood run cold. She felt her freedom slipping away.

Her dad followed her to the door, and she opened it, her heart pounding in her chest. A young woman stood on the porch, a white rose in her fingers. She wore the traditional clothing of the lynx females, a white peasant blouse and a full skirt.

"King Maurice wishes you a happy twenty-third birthday tomorrow, Reika Snow. You have twenty-four hours to say goodbye to your family. At sunset tomorrow, your husbands will be waiting for you. You may bring two bags."

Reika took the rose, bile rising in her throat, and watched the woman turn and walk down the steps of the porch, down the sidewalk to the street, where a truck waited for her.

"Twenty-four hours," her mother said sadly. "I had so hoped you might find your truemate, sweetheart."

"I know, Mom."

They spent the rest of the evening together, with a pall cast over what would have been a normally cheerful, casual evening. Ben had tossed the rose into the outside trashcan immediately, but its presence still lingered in the house like a ghost.

Reika had packed the night before, one duffel bag containing two changes of clothes, toiletries, and her dog-eared copy of her favorite book, *The Princess Bride*.

She prepared two letters. One to her parents to tell them she was leaving but would be safe from the lynxes, and that in the future, when it was safe for her, she would contact them. The other letter was for Ben, so he understood she didn't hold him responsible for what had happened and that she loved him.

When the hour grew late, she kissed her family goodnight as she always did, taking a mental picture of her parents cuddled together on the couch in front of the fire and her brother as he made cinnamon rolls in the kitchen for tomorrow's breakfast—his Friday night ritual. She struggled not to cry, not to say goodbye and tell them her plans. But it was far safer for them to remain ignorant of what she was doing.

She didn't dare sleep. She had to leave at 12:30 a.m. in order to walk to the rental car she stashed behind a gas station, two miles from her home. It would take her approximately four hours to drive to the Louisville Airport.

Her parents went to bed at eleven, and her brother followed shortly. She heard them all moving around in their rooms as she sat on the edge of her bed and watched the clock. Finally, the house was silent. She dressed warmly, sprayed heavy perfume all over herself to mask her scent in case anyone tried to follow her through the woods at any time, left the two letters on her bed, and opened the window of her second-story bedroom. She dropped gracefully and silently, rolling in the snow and popping up onto her feet.

The two miles through the wooded area between the neighboring streets concealed her as she ran in near darkness, spilling out onto the main street and darting across an empty intersection where her rental car waited. The WAA had reserved it for her. She had picked the car up on Tuesday and parked it behind a deserted gas station.

She kept a sharp eye on her mirrors and drove as fast as she dared. She was positive that no one had followed her. Her frayed nerves and the thought of what would happen if the lynxes caught her fleeing kept her alert in spite of how little sleep she'd gotten during the week.

Almost free, she thought, as she pulled into the parking lot of the airport and walked to the American Airlines terminal. She looked around, scanning the nearly empty airport for anyone who looked familiar, and saw no one she recognized. Two men, wearing military-style pants and black jackets, stepped into view and motioned for her.

"R. S.?" the taller of the two said.

"Yes."

"Do you have your cell, computer, or any form of ID?" the other asked.

"No." She'd taken a chance on driving without her license and left it at home, knowing that she would have had to toss it out once she arrived at the airport.

"Good. Here is your new identification. Your name is now Brittany Caulfield. Our flight is preparing to board. Let's go." The taller one held out a driver's license to her, and as she reached for it, a piercing roar ripped through the silence around them.

She darted her eyes around the terminal as the two wolves put their hands on her arms, urging her to follow them to the gate. The wolves were knocked away from her by three hulking figures who snarled warnings in deep, guttural words. She hadn't seen Eli, Josef, and Adam for sixteen years, but she recognized them immediately. They threw the wolves around as though they were stuffed toys. The taller wolf went through a glass wall and hit the outside sidewalk hard. Josef hauled the other wolf over his head and threw him into the courtesy desk with a sickening crack.

Regaining her senses, she raced out an exit just as the airport security came running to the scene. She waved frantically at a taxi that was about to pull away. When it stopped, she jerked open the back door, threw herself inside, and slammed the door.

"Where to, honey?" a woman driver said.

"Anywhere! Just get me out of here!" Reika panted.

The car pulled away quickly, and Reika watched out the back window as Eli, Josef, and Adam ran out of the building and looked around. Their eyes locked on hers, and she knew they had seen her in the taxi. She was glad for the momentary reprieve when police cars with flashing lights pulled up in front of the terminal and she saw the lynxes scatter.

As the scene faded into the distance, she knew that they would only be temporarily detained from finding her. They would maim and kill anyone who came between her and them; she could see that clearly now. She had no idea how they followed her, except that they must have been watching her home.

Saying a silent prayer for the two wolves who fell trying to help her, she took in a deep breath and focused on her situation. She faced the front of the taxi and looked at the middle-aged woman.

"Can you take me an hour south and drop me off somewhere public and well-lit? And push the speed limit, please."

"You in trouble, honey?" The woman met Reika's eyes in the rear-view mirror as she pressed her foot on the gas.

"I don't know," Reika answered honestly.

She didn't imagine her bid for freedom potentially costing two men their lives, and she hoped they had survived and she would, too.

Chapter Two

Bo fidgeted in the booth at Jake's bar, his hazel gaze roaming over the Friday night regulars. He was positively bored stupid. He'd rather be cleaning his house than sitting in the bar. There wasn't a damn thing to do in Allen on Friday night except hang out at Jake's, and it was the responsibility of the older wolves in the pack to make sure the younger wolves kept their heads on straight. Alcohol lowered inhibitions, which in a human was not necessarily a bad thing. But add in the ability to shift into a werewolf, and a few beers could turn a mild-mannered person into a raging beast.

Bo drank, but only to dull the pain in his right leg. The effects of the alcohol were working less and less, though, which was good news for his liver, but not for his leg. Nights spent walking the floor in an effort to stretch out the cramped muscles meant he was exhausted more often than not.

Logan, fifth ranked in the pack, sat across from him and stared into the bottom of the tumbler that was half-full of whiskey. Logan had joined the pack a few months ago in the summer, and he was proving to be a good wolf to know.

Bo was going to be thirty on March 1. He hadn't really thought he would be in his late twenties and not mated to some hot, little she-wolf, but here he was … alone on a Friday night.

Running a hand through his short, black hair, he sighed and checked his watch. It was nearly midnight, and tomorrow was the full moon. Each full moon, one of the high-ranked wolves watched over the younger wolves who were responsible for cleaning and preparing their full moon gathering place for their celebration.

Normally, Bo watched over the younger wolves during the summer months because the cold aggravated his leg, but it was Linus and his mate Karly's anniversary, and he'd asked for a favor, so Bo was stuck.

He could call his alpha, Jason, and tell him that his leg was bothering him too much. He knew Jason would tell him to take it easy and call another wolf to do it, or even do it himself, but Bo refused to give into the pain like that. If he couldn't handle sweeping off snow and unloading firewood, then he needed to step down from his rank. And damn it, he'd worked too hard to roll over like that.

Eventually, though, his leg would force him to stop shifting, and then he'd have to step down. He didn't look forward to that day, and he felt as if a blade hung over his neck, ready to cut him off sooner than he wanted.

"Hey, Bo," a sugary voice drawled in his ear, and he cringed inwardly.

Schooling his face, he took a drink of beer and looked up at Lindy, one of the pack females. She was the same age as their alpha female, Cadence, who was a hybrid human-wolf, and married to Jason. He could smell lust rolling off Lindy, and underneath that, the chemical smell of her bleached-blonde hair and heavy, floral perfume.

"Hi, Lindy."

He didn't offer her more than that, because he knew what she wanted. She was what the pack referred to as a Toy—a she-wolf who would have sex with any wolf, any time. When he was younger and she wasn't so jaded and used up, he'd tumbled with her. But not in a long time.

She cleared her throat, her lustful smile losing its brightness. "I thought you might like to," she leaned down toward his ear and whispered, "take me home with you."

Logan arched a brow at him but said nothing. Bo was a little surprised by her boldness, but then again she'd been trying to fuck her way into a mating with a highly ranked male for the last few months, and so far, that hadn't seemed to work out too well for her.

Her hand landed on his shoulder, and he lifted it off. "Sorry, full moon duty tomorrow."

She stuck out her lip and pouted. "Aw, maybe tomorrow then, lover?"

Be nice or not? He debated. Better to get it over with, like ripping off a Band-Aid. "Sorry, Lindy. But thanks anyway."

Her lip curled into an unpleasant sneer, and embarrassment heated her cheeks. She turned on her heel and stormed off, probably going to console herself with another, more desperate, wolf. He felt sorry for her. There was a time when he thought of her as sweet and innocent, but that certainly didn't describe her anymore.

Logan snorted, and Bo looked at him. "What?"

Logan swirled the ice in his glass. "You said *thanks*."

Confused, Bo asked, "What should I have said?"

Logan didn't smile much, but he did now. "She offered to fuck you, and you said *thanks anyway*. Like she offered to knit you a sweater or something. It's just—I don't know, man, kinda funny."

Bo scowled. He didn't think it was rude to say thanks, but maybe in that situation, he should have just told her flat-out no. Oh well. Maybe now she wouldn't keep asking him, since he'd apparently insulted her.

"You're just jealous," Bo said and grinned. Logan wanted to find his mate, as much as Bo did, but for both of them, their mates weren't in the Tressel pack. Which sucked, considering that it wasn't as if Bo ran across a she-wolf from another pack every day.

"I don't think so. I'll find my mate someday, and she won't be a Toy who throws herself at everyone, either." Logan finished his drink with two swallows and set the empty glass down.

"I feel the same way." Bo tilted his beer back and finished it, ready to put a fork in the evening.

After stopping by the back of the bar to say goodbye to his former alphas, Peter and Tina, who were Jason's parents, he climbed into his pickup, waved goodbye to Logan, who had walked out with him, and headed home.

Two years earlier, the Tressel pack had shared Allen, Kentucky with the Garra pack. The son of the alpha of the Garra pack had kidnapped and tried to rape Cadence, Jason's wife. When the Tressel pack delivered pack justice to the son of the alpha and his cohorts, four wolves were dead. The Garra pack left Allen shortly after and headed South, and they turned over the deeds to their homes to the Tressel pack. Anyone who wanted to take over the paid-for, older homes, could do so easily. Allen was a small town, and between the active pack members and retired pack members, the town was about fifty-percent wolf, and the pack really wanted to keep it that way.

Bo had paid a fee to the bank in order to purchase the deed to the home of one of the wolves from the Garra Pack. Before that, he'd lived in a single-wide in the back corner of Allen's trailer park. It had been easy enough to unload the trailer on one of the younger wolves, who was eager to move out of his parents' home after he turned eighteen.

Tossing his keys on the kitchen table, Bo pulled off his jacket, hung it over a chair, and yawned. He remembered when he used to think that midnight was early. Not so much anymore.

Flopping on his king-size bed, he closed his eyes and prayed that his leg wouldn't wake him up. *Just one night*, he thought. *I just need one fucking good night's sleep.*

The dream came to him again, and he was caught in his past, the moment when his life skewed in a shitty direction, and everything he ever planned for his life went to hell.

He'd skipped school before, so when he overheard his older brother, Mack, telling a buddy that they were going to sneak into the old theater in the next town and watch an R-rated movie, Bo decided to follow and join in. Mack was three years older than Bo, and Bo idolized him. Seventeen year-old Mack had everything that Bo wanted at the tender age of fourteen—he was one of the strongest wolves in his age group, he had a fast car and a fast she-wolf on his arm.

That day, Bo snuck out after lunch period and walked from the high school down to the bus station and caught a bus to Greystone, where Mack and his friends were going to sneak into the Busman Theater. As he stepped from the bus station and walked four blocks down to the old theater, he caught sight of his brother and friends as they ducked into the alley between the theater and the grocery next door.

Bo didn't think about the danger as he stepped down into the street; he simply stepped out and started jogging. He heard a shout and the blast of a horn, turning in time to see a car barreling down on him. He heard the breaks squeal as the driver stomped on them. Bo remembered throwing his arms up to protect his face as the car rammed into him, knocking him onto the asphalt.

He remembered the rush of wind as he was thrown twenty feet from the car and the sound of the first crunch of bone as he slammed into the pavement, and then everything went black. He woke up several days later in the hospital, fighting against incredible pain, because of his hopelessly mangled leg.

His parents told him he was lucky to be alive. Although too young to shift into his wolf form by two years, he still had an accelerated healing ability that, in fact, had saved his life. A human would have been killed. He hadn't felt very lucky when the pain meds didn't work because there were none that would for a wolf. He'd brought his fate on himself by doing something he wasn't supposed to do. One wrong choice had effectively changed his life forever.

The numerous surgeries helped, and when he was able to shift at sixteen, his body naturally healed what it could, but the damage had been done. Along with an ugly scar—left behind by the surgeries—that wove down his right leg; the muscles were also damaged, and his joints ached constantly. It was a dull, insistent pain that he could ignore on most days. Some days, though, it made him want to cut his leg off and be done with the pain.

He was awake well before dawn, either the past rearing its ugly head again via the dream, or the pain in his leg, keeping him from the deep, restful sleep he so desperately needed. Sleeping pills didn't work on wolves; otherwise he would happily addict himself to find a way to sleep.

What was worse, Bo thought, was that his libido had seemed to take a long-term vacation. The last few months he couldn't get it up for anyone, and two months ago while one of the she-wolves had been blowing him in the storage room at the bar, his cock hadn't so much as twitched. First his leg and then his cock. He just couldn't catch a break.

He watched the handful of young teen wolves sweep the snow from the circle where the pack would gather on the full moon to shift and hunt together as one. The clearing was a few hundred yards behind Jason and Cadence's home. Michael and his human mate, Shyne, lived in the home next door.

After downing the last of his coffee, Bo began hauling firewood into the freshly cleared pit that would be lit when the sun set. His thoughts wandered, and his wolf came to his mind, the furry beast growling lightly. Pausing, Bo tapped into his beast and felt as if a change was coming. The change could be anything, even just a storm. But still … Bo was beginning to feel that something might happen tonight. He just hoped to hell it was something good.

When the work was done, Bo sent the wolves to Jason's house to ask if there was anything else the alpha needed, and then he headed home himself.

That night, as the moon rose in the sky, Jason called for the pack to shift and hunt, and Bo watched as the wolves around him shed their clothes and shifted into their wolf forms. Bo didn't get naked in front of anybody except doctors. He couldn't stand to see the pity, especially from women, when they saw his leg. Even when he had sex he always kept his pants on.

Jason, Michael, Linus, and Logan looked at him after they shifted and then turned and padded into the woods. They gave him privacy without being obvious about it, and he appreciated it. Alone, he stripped and shifted quickly, his bones cracking and muscles aching as he changed into his dark grey form. Shaking out his body, he grimaced at the twinge of pain in his leg. When he was younger, shifting gave him some relief from the constant hum of pain in his leg, but lately, relief escaped him. Pain had become a permanent part of his life.

He trotted off after his friends. As he neared the group, Linus caught a scent and darted off, barking sharply to encourage the rest of them to follow. Bo caught the scent of deer a few moments later as they raced through the woods to find their prey.

Something else caught Bo's attention, and he skidded to a halt, the snow fluffing up around his legs. He turned and scented further, finding an enticing aroma coming from far in the distance. Whatever it was, he had to have it.

As he raced towards the scent, he heard his friends barking at him in question, but he ignored them. The woods rushed past him, the familiar surroundings of their pack territory morphing into unfamiliar woods.

He paused, scenting, and found blood on the wind and a faint echo of fear that caused his heart to speed up as he took off again. Whatever he would find was injured and afraid. This creature, whatever it was, was now the single most important thing in his life.

Crashing through a dense thicket, he halted as he came upon three cats—lynxes by the looks of the black tufts on their ears—who circled a she-wolf. They were just slightly smaller than him, buffed gold and covered with black spots. A wound gaped from the she-wolf's side, dripping dark red blood onto the white snow. The three males circled her, snapping their teeth and snagging bits of her hide. She whimpered and lashed at them, her eyes wide with fear.

Bo's hackles rose as he watched the she-wolf hold her own in a severely outnumbered battle, and he barked sharply to insert himself into the fight. She needed a champion, and he was just the wolf for the job. The three males turned to look at him and then turned back to her, hissing and growling. Bo realized the she-wolf was the one whose scent was calling for him. He didn't take time to consider what it meant; only that she was in danger and needed to be saved. With a sharp howl, he stalked towards the three as the female struck out weakly, her fangs bared in fury.

Two of the lynxes crouched, ready to spring on the female, and the third, who she didn't see, slipped behind her. As they'd planned, she turned to race away from the two and ran straight into the third, who snagged her scruff in his jaws and shook her hard, her teeth snapping together, until her body went limp.

Bo didn't stop to consider the consequences of his actions; he simply acted. Roaring in rage at the treatment of the female, he leapt at the male who held her, smashing into his side. The lynx released the she-wolf with a surprised grunt as he tumbled to the ground beneath Bo. Moving quickly, Bo grabbed the lynx's back leg in his jaws and jerked him further away from the she-wolf. The lynxes had not considered him a threat; that was their mistake. Bo crouched protectively in front of the injured female and snapped at the other two. They circled him, growling low, but he didn't back down, daring them, with growls and snapping jaws, to come closer.

The lynx righted himself, shook the snow from his back, and growled a warning to Bo. But Bo wasn't going anywhere without the woman who had suddenly come to mean everything to him. *She's mine!* He growled and lowered his head, preparing for their attack and planning his counter-attack. He wasn't third-ranked for nothing. He had fought and trained his whole life so that his leg didn't stop him from being the best. These cats could go to hell.

The lynxes eyed him warily, casting glances back and forth. After staring at him for a long moment, the one who Bo had tackled growled sharply, and the lynxes turned as a group and padded away. Bo held his rigid, protective stance until he could no longer see or hear them. Then he relaxed, but only slightly, turning his attention to the wounded female in the snow. Nudging her gently with his nose, he listened for her heartbeat and found it weak and her breathing shallow. He shifted into his human form and carefully picked her up.

His truck was still at the full moon clearing. From his best guess, he was several miles away. He walked as fast as his leg would allow, ignoring the pain and the cold, and concentrated on the slight form in his arms. Beautiful inky, blue-hued black fur covered her body.

He'd never seen a wolf colored like her. Jason's family line was black, but not like this. Whoever she was, she faced down a group of three lynxes alone. If they hadn't tricked her, she might have escaped.

Exhaustion plagued Bo—physically and mentally—but that didn't stop his brain from trying to process everything he'd seen. Three male cats had attacked a lone she-wolf. He'd never seen a were-lynx before, and he sure hoped to hell he wouldn't see those three anytime soon.

He couldn't deny that there was something about her. Something that called to him. All he knew for certain was that he was going to take care of her for however long she would allow.

The full moon clearing was empty as he'd expected. Wolves only stayed in their shift for a few hours on the full moon, until they sated their need to run and hunt. The pack would have come back to the clearing, shifted, and left. Some of the pack, the younger, single males and females, would head to someone's home and hang out. Casual hookups were normal on full moon nights.

A thin layer of snow covered his truck. With his leg burning as though hot pokers were shoved beneath the skin, he put the female inside his truck, dressed, and drove home.

He carried the unconscious woman, still in her wolf form, into his bedroom and laid her on his bed, pulling a thick comforter over her. Her fur was chilled, her ears ice cold. Bo opened the hall closet and pulled extra blankets from the shelves, stopping to kick up the heat in the house. When he returned to the bedroom, she had shifted to her human form. She shivered uncontrollably, but remained unconscious. He laid the blankets on the end of the bed and went into the bathroom to grab a first-aid kit.

He pulled the blanket back gently so he could tend her wounds. Seeing her injuries made his breath catch in his throat, and his wolf howled for revenge in his mind.

One of the lynx's claws had torn a jagged gash from under her arm to the curve of her waist. He cleansed the wound carefully with antiseptic pads from the kit, grateful the gash had stopped bleeding and was starting to heal. He covered the large wound on her side with gauze pads and tape and tended her other scratches and scrapes. Her ivory skin was covered with bruises and scrapes, and as he gently tested her joints and bones for breaks, his rage grew.

Once he finished, he laid the comforter on top of her and then covered her with every blanket in the house. With a warm, wet cloth, he carefully cleaned her face of dirt and dried blood and was astonished to see how beautiful she was. Even injured, she was simply stunning. He rubbed at his leg and looked at her, wondering what her name was and how she had gotten into trouble with the lynxes.

After an hour, except for her shivers going away as she warmed up, she hadn't moved or made a sound. He didn't know what else to do.

Picking up his cell, Bo stepped out of the bedroom and called his Aunt Lia. She was human and dabbled in wicca healing because she didn't believe in Western medicine. Lia married his uncle, who was a wolf and had died in a car crash several years earlier. Lia lived on the outskirts of town and made house calls for people who didn't want to go a traditional doctor.

Bo told her what had happened, and his aunt agreed to come right away. Half an hour later when she walked into Bo's bedroom, Lia took one look at the woman and made clucking noises in her mouth. She checked the woman's vitals and hummed in her throat as Bo stood protectively nearby. Even though it was his aunt, Bo didn't like anyone else's hands on the woman. Lia pulled the blankets aside and lifted the bandage, looking at the deep wound. From a small bag she had brought, Lia pulled a vial and two clean, white cloths. She opened the vial and soaked one cloth with clear oil that smelled herbal but not any herbs he could place. Lia gently pressed the cloth onto the large wound and then covered it with fresh bandages and secured it to the woman's side with tape from the first-aid kit. Wetting the other cloth, she rubbed the oil on the other cuts.

Almost reverently, Lia placed the blankets on top of the woman and turned to him. "Do you know anything about lynxes, Bo?"

He shook his head. "I've never even seen one before. If I hadn't recognized the fur tufts on their ears, I might have thought they were some kind of leopard. Why? What do you know about them?"

"Do you remember my friend Ada? She lived in Phoenix for a while, and she told me that a group of lynxes came through their town once a year. They're like the gypsies of the shifter world. They don't stay in one place too long, and they trade for what they need. They also make arranged marriages."

He stiffened and looked down at the woman in his bed. Was she promised to those males who hurt her? *Not for long*, his wolf growled in his mind.

"You said her coloring was unique. It's possible, and I'm just guessing here from the things Ada told me, that her parents promised her to one or all of those males as some kind of arranged marriage. Maybe to form an alliance, or maybe in payment for something the lynxes did. You'll have to wait until she wakes up to find out her situation. Whatever the reason, though, the fact that they injured her so badly in an effort to subdue her doesn't speak well to their intentions, or what her life would be like if she went back to them."

"What can I do for her?"

Lia looked up at him, and Bo couldn't quite decipher her expression. Pride and something else. "She'll need to sleep until her body is healed. When she wakes, she may be terrified. There's no way to know what she remembers. I can take care of her, if you want me to take over for you."

His wolf snapped angrily. *She's mine!* "No! I mean, no thank you, Aunt Lia, I'll handle it."

She smiled, rose from the bed, and returned the empty vial to her bag. "The oil I put on will help her wound heal, aiding her natural healing ability. Treat her well and take care of her, Bo. I know you'll do just fine."

He kissed her cheek. "Thanks."

"Call me tomorrow, and let me know how things are going. If she's really been given to those males, I doubt they'll let go of her so easily. If they chased her here, then they possibly have a way to find her no matter where she is. Please be careful."

Bo saw Lia out and locked the door. He stood next to the woman on his bed, brushing a lock of hair away from her face. Her ivory skin complemented her delicate features. Dark hair fell like an obsidian curtain, pooling on the pillow beneath her head. She had an adorable nose, pink lips, and ears that looked just right for nibbling and whispering tantalizing desires. He hadn't exactly been able to ignore how her bare body looked as he'd tended her wounds. Full breasts, skin that looked as soft as satin, flat belly, and perfectly flared hips. He wondered what color her eyes were.

Thinking about those lynxes who had been attacking her made his hackles rise. If what Lia said was true, and her family had promised her to them, the fact that she was running from them spoke volumes. She should get to choose who she mated with, and Bo didn't only believe that because she was gorgeous and caused his wolf to desire to claim her. Not that she'd want him. He was broken, after all. What female of worth in her right mind would choose a wolf who would be out of commission in a few years due to a bad leg? And he didn't even want to think what their love life might be like once the pain overtook him. No, she deserved better than he could ever be.

But what he could do for her was help her get free of whatever claim those lynxes had on her. Based on his aunt's information, the lynxes wouldn't be afraid of losing her because they could track her somehow. Perhaps by her scent.

Bo left her and made himself a few sandwiches while he called Jason. It was still early in the morning, and he knew that Jason would still be in bed, like most wolves, sleeping in the day after the full moon.

Jason answered on the second ring, sounding hoarse and groggy. Bo apologized for waking him, and then explained what happened, finishing the story by adding that he might have led an angry group of lynxes to town.

"That's a hell of a thing, Bo," Jason said finally. "But I always knew you were noble."

Bo snorted. "Thanks, man."

"Look," Jason said evenly, "if they come to town looking for her and she doesn't want to be found, the pack will back you up. They can probably track her by scent, but your trail would have ended at the circle. If they come to town to ask about her or you, we'll send them on their way."

"Thanks."

"Hey, if her people just gave her away to another shifter group and she doesn't want that, then I think it's a shit thing, and she's more than welcome to sanctuary in our territory for however long she needs it. Besides, once I tell Cades what happened, you know she's going to rally the females to her cause. If the lynxes think you're worth backing down from in a fight, they haven't seen my wife when she's pissed off. They don't stand a chance." Jason laughed, and Bo joined in. Cadence might only be half wolf and unable to shift, but she was all alpha, right down to the very core.

"Is she about Cades' size? I can send some clothes over," Jason offered.

Bo hadn't even thought about what she would wear when she woke up. "That would be great. If they don't fit, at least they'll do until I can get her something else."

"Alright. Keep in touch, and let me know if you need anything at all."

Bo ended the call, proud that he could count on his friend and alpha. He hadn't expected less. He went into the master bathroom and took a shower, letting the hot water work on his sore muscles. He'd been up for more than twenty-four hours now, and he was damn tired. After rubbing a numbing ointment onto his bad leg, he pulled on a pair of jeans and sat down in the leather chair in the corner of the bedroom.

As he settled himself to rest, he made a vow to himself and to the woman in the bed. Today was the start of his new life. He'd been dealt a shit hand in life with his injury, but he'd never been forcibly mated before, chased down by another group when he was weak and wounded.

The woman needed help, and Bo was going to do anything in his power to set her free from those who would harm her. He would keep her safe.

Chapter Three

Sleep eluded Reika, slipping away like a shadow being chased by the sun, and although she tried to hold onto it, she couldn't. And then she remembered that she wasn't supposed to be asleep; she was supposed to be running for her life.

Her eyes snapped open, and she bolted upright, her blurry vision taking in everything too fast for her to process. Rubbing her eyes with her palms, she blinked several times and scanned the room. She wasn't racing through unfamiliar woods at night with the lynxes hot on her tail. This was someone's home. And that someone was seated in a chair in a corner, slumped down and fast asleep.

Reika knew him immediately by his scent as the events of last night replayed through her mind quickly. He was the male wolf she had seen before she was rendered unconscious by one of the lynx's harsh actions. The wolf had clearly come to her aid. But what happened to the lynxes? Dare she hope that they were dead and out of her life forever? Although her luck had improved considerably with the wolf who had saved her, she doubted the wolf spirits liked her enough to kill off the lynxes, too.

She remembered the taxi had driven her for an hour and dropped her off at an all-night car rental. Using her new ID, she rented the first car available, tossed her bag in the back, and drove. She had no idea where she was, but she could practically feel the lynxes on her tail even though she never actually saw anyone. She sped, turning down various streets. She pulled the car into a park when the gas tank was nearly empty. It was near dusk. She saw a truck moving slowly down the park's main drive, the same truck that had picked up the young woman with the rose on her birthday. With her heart pounding, she looked around frantically for help but saw no people or open businesses. She had only one chance to escape, and that was to shift and run.

She stripped, tucked the keys into the visor, left her bag under the passenger seat, shifted, and raced off. The full moon loomed in the sky, and Reika ran quickly for as long as she could. She could feel she wasn't alone. She felt the menace and hatred emanating from the lynxes. They weren't going to take her nicely. They were pissed she'd run.

She ran as far and as fast as she could, but they caught up to her, trying to injure her so she couldn't run anymore. She remembered them striking out at her, wounding her. She closed her eyes against the memories and shook them away.

Reika would never be able to hide from the lynxes. They had excellent scenting abilities. She had no idea how they'd found her in the airport in the first place, but it didn't matter. If the wolf who had saved her had chased them off, it was only because the lynxes knew they would be able to find her again, no matter where she was. She shivered in the bed.

The only thing Reika could do was keep running. One problem was that she was out of money. Her belongings were in the rental car in the park, and she had no idea where the car even was.

She looked at the man. If he had saved her life, could he help her escape? There had to be a place she could go where the lynxes would never find her, or he could perhaps help her contact the WAA again.

Reika noticed he was handsome. Thick black hair cut short and carelessly mussed, tan skin, stubble-darkened jaw, and a mouth made for kissing, with a slightly larger lower lip that just begged to be nibbled. As she let her eyes roam over him shamelessly while he slept, she noticed his features shift slowly, from peaceful and smooth to frowning and drawn. His brows drew together, his lips pressed into a thin line, and his body went rigid.

"No, no," he murmured, lost to his bad dreams. His hands tightened slightly and his body jerked.

Reika couldn't stand to watch him suffer in his nightmare, so she pulled the sheet around herself and straightened from the bed, wincing at a tugging pain in her side. She moved to him, kneeling and laying one hand on his arm.

His eyes popped open immediately, hazel and bottomless.

"You shouldn't be up, sweetheart. You've got a bad gash on your side," he said, his deep voice rumbling pleasantly in her ears. His jaw was clenched tight, and his knuckles were white, but his body remained relaxed so he managed to look at ease. She guessed he was doing that for her benefit.

"I do?" She blinked up at him. She parted the sheet to reveal where the pain radiated. She pulled away a bandage, and saw three claw marks that were healing.

Shaking her head slightly at the wound, she said, "You were having a nightmare. Are you okay?"

His eyes rested on her, warmth in the depths, and he pressed his palm to her cheek. "I'm not the one who was attacked by three males last night."

With a quick motion, he scooped her up in his arms and set her back on the bed, squatting on the floor in front of her. "Can I get you anything?"

"Your name?"

"Ah, sorry." He smiled, and she had a feeling that he didn't smile much, or he hadn't smiled in a long time. She liked his smile, though. Took him from handsome to gorgeous in 2.2 seconds. "My name is Bo Elliott."

"I'm Reika Snow. Thank you for saving me."

He told her the story of how he'd followed her scent and stumbled into the middle of the lynxes trying to subdue her. She clutched the blanket to herself in shame. It must all seem so barbaric to him.

"Hey, hey," he chided softly, "I don't give a damn what their reasons were. You're a person and not property to be treated so poorly." He stood slowly and winced, but schooled his features quickly to hide the pain that temporarily marred his features. Her healing nature told her that something was wrong with one leg, something old, and that he had been tormented with nightmares from the injury ever since.

"Thank you, Bo."

"I'm glad I was there, Reika."

She liked the way he said her name. Like a verbal caress. She chided herself for thinking such sweet things about the man. He was her hero, sure, but she needed to hit the road quick so she didn't bring hell to whatever town she'd landed in.

"What day is it?" The early sunlight told her it was morning, but she had a feeling she had been sleeping longer than just a few hours.

"It's Monday morning. I found you late Saturday night, and you've been asleep since I brought you here and you shifted."

She nodded, chewing on her bottom lip. Had the males come for her already or were they biding their time?

Bo placed his hand gently on her bare shoulder. "You're safe here, Reika. I swear on my life."

His words were as honest and genuine as any she'd ever heard. This was an honorable wolf, and he was promising to keep her safe. A well of emotion threatened to open up inside her, and she swallowed hard, fighting not to fall apart.

Reika looked down at her hands that clutched the sheet to her body and noticed her fingernails were caked with dirt. "I must look awful. Can I take a shower?"

"You look perfect, Reika. But of course you can," Bo said with a smile as he helped her stand. He showed her the bathroom. "My female alpha brought over some clothes for you last night and some, uh, girly things. When you're done, I'll have breakfast for you."

Leaving her no time to respond, Bo left her in the bathroom, and she shut the door, turning the shower on and dropping the sheet. Steeling herself, she looked into the mirror over the sink and sucked in a breath. Bruises and scrapes dotted her flesh, overshadowed only by the angry claw marks on her side. Thankful for her fast healing, she stepped under the spray and cleaned up.

Reika was warmed through and through by Bo's sweet words, but what could he really do about a lynx clan that was intent on having her as mate for its males and as a healer for its warriors? She could sense that Bo was powerful, most likely highly ranked in his pack, but that didn't mean she wanted him to take his pack to war for her.

She couldn't remember ever waking up and not feeling her impending mating to the lynx males hanging over her head. But she'd woken up feeling safe with Bo. Her wolf growled softly in her mind. She felt attracted to him. Not just physically, but deeper. She stopped her mind from exploring the growing attraction to the handsome wolf before it went too far.

Sighing, she turned off the shower and got out, wrapping a thick towel around herself. Bo wouldn't want her. She was damaged goods. Arranged to be married to three lynx males. The only way that Bo could break that bond was if he was her truemate. And even then, he would have to fight all three males for the right to mate her.

How did she start that conversation? *I feel connected to you, cutie. How would you like to risk your life for a woman you just met?*

No, it was better to just be on her way as fast as possible. That was best, for all their sakes.

His alpha female had left a stack of clothes of different sizes, and she chose a pair of comfortable jeans and a thick, soft sweater. The underwear was in a new package, and the bra was a new sports bra.

She brushed her teeth and hair, took one last look at herself in the mirror, and stepped out into the bedroom. The scent of bacon called to her, and she followed it to a cozy kitchen. Bo, now wearing a long sleeved shirt with his jeans, stood at the stove, using a fork to remove bacon from a pan.

"Ouch, shit," he groused, wiping his hand after grease snapped up at him.

She smiled. "It's nice to see a man who knows his way around a kitchen."

Bo looked over his shoulder, his eyes brightening when he saw her. "Don't get too excited. I can only do the basics. Bacon, eggs, boiling water."

He returned his attention to the bacon, finished removing the slices from the pan, and turned off the burner. Setting the hot pan on a cool burner, he said, "Have a seat, Reika."

She sat down on one of the two chairs at the pub table, as he put down a plate of bacon alongside a stack of toaster-heated waffles, a bowl of scrambled eggs, and a pot of coffee. "I know this isn't all that great, but I wasn't sure when you would wake up, so I just had one of the wolves bring me some things I could throw together easily."

"It's perfect, Bo, really. Thank you."

She turned her attention to the waffles, putting two on her plate and smothering them with butter and syrup. She sweetened her coffee and added a splash of milk, taking an experimental sip before deciding it was perfect.

"So ... where am I?" she asked after taking a bite of waffle.

"Allen."

"Is that in Kentucky?" She'd never heard of the town before, and she had no idea where she'd been when she stopped in the park or how long she'd run in her shift.

He frowned. "Yes. Where are you from? Is there someone you'd like to call? Your family?"

Her heart panged in her chest. She desperately wanted to call her parents, but she didn't dare. What if the lynxes had their people watching her house? She couldn't risk her parents knowing anything.

She'd never really been a good liar, but the less that Bo knew about her, the better. "There isn't anyone to call."

She busied herself eating, feeling dejected at not only lying to him, but also pretending as if her family didn't exist.

He didn't ask any follow-up questions, and she was grateful. They ate in silence, but she could feel him watching her. She found it incredibly arousing but tried to banish the lustful thoughts from her mind.

When they were finished eating and the plates were washed and set in the drainer, he dried his hands off on a kitchen towel and led her to the overstuffed tan suede couch. She sat and sunk down into a cushion.

Bo paced for a bit, and there was a definite hitch in his gait. She zeroed in on his right leg. She knew her initial healing senses had been right. His leg was badly injured. For a wolf, that was bad news. It meant that either he had been too young to shift and heal himself, or he hadn't been able to shift to help himself heal correctly.

He eased down onto the coffee table and rubbed at his thigh. His movements stilled when he noticed she watched him, and embarrassment flushed his cheeks.

Clearing his throat, he said, "So, want to tell me why three lynxes tried to kidnap you?"

Right to the point, of course.

"I, um," she started, unsure of whether she should tell him anything or just leave.

"Listen, Reika, it's pretty clear that you were running from them, and they're not the sort of males who are above seriously injuring a female. I saved you, and I just want to know what I'm getting myself involved in, so I can figure out how best to move forward."

"What? You don't have to get yourself involved in anything." She stood. "Thank you for saving me, Bo, but you don't need to get mixed up in the shit I'm eyeball deep in."

He pushed himself from the coffee table, standing more than half a foot taller than her 5'5" frame, and gripped her arms. His fingers flexed lightly, restraining but not hurting. "I'm not the sort of male who rescues a woman in distress and then lets her go on her merry way, so get that thought far from your mind. I'll help you in whatever way you need so you're free. You'll stay here, with me, until that happens."

Reika opened her mouth to protest, but the determination in Bo's eyes told her that she could argue for a week, but it wouldn't make a difference. He had no intention of just letting her walk away. She dropped her head as tears of relief mingled with worry—worry that she would never really be safe, worry that she had brought hell into Allen, and worry that Bo would get hurt or killed trying to keep her, a stranger, safe.

Not a stranger, her wolf seemed to growl, *mate.*

Bo took in a surprised breath, and she heard the answering growl of his wolf. She lifted her head slowly, following the broad chest and shoulders up to the perfectly kissable lips that parted ever so slightly as he panted. Arousal—both of theirs—filled the air around them. She could drown in it. Gladly.

But then reality slapped her in the face, and she remembered the three lynxes who were intent on taking her.

She knocked his hands away from her arms and stepped back, putting the couch between them. Reigning in the tight desire that swamped her, she told him what had happened, from Ben's accident to the rose at her front door to the WAA to the males catching her in the woods.

Bo cracked his knuckles, anger marring his handsome features. His eyes flashed, from hazel to amber, and her first thought was that he was the sort of male she had dreamed would take her away, save her from the lynxes' promise, and be hers forever. But reality was too brutal to contemplate the safety that he promised her. No matter how well intentioned, one male wolf was no match for three determined lynxes. She knew that. He had to know that, too. But wolves could be stubborn and equally determined. She didn't want his determination to get him killed.

"You're not going anywhere, Reika. You'll stay here with me until we get you free of the promise to those males. And you really should call your family and let them know what happened. I'm sure they're worried about you."

He moved to her and reached out, tucking a lock of hair behind her ear. The feather-light touch made her shiver all over. His concern, coupled with the thought of her family suffering, made the dam break loose, and she fell into his arms and wept.

He held her tightly, stroking her hair and murmuring soft, soothing things to her. Reika let go of all the tears she'd held in for so long concerning the situation, and she cried new tears thinking about her family's suffering and how her situation had drawn a kind, amazing man into the middle of the disaster that was her life.

She cried until she couldn't cry anymore, and Bo never wavered, never stopped stroking her, talking to her, holding her. Reika felt right with him. Safe. Cared for. And drawn to him … *so* drawn to him. Her body tensed as the word she'd tried to ignore pounded through her mind again.

Mate.

Bo … a male who had run to her in her time of need, drawn only by the scent of her fear, was her truemate. The one male capable of setting her free. And the one male who she now wanted to protect more than anyone.

She wouldn't ask him to fight for her, and she wouldn't let him know that she was aware they were mates. She would keep him at arm's length until she could find a way out of here, and she'd leave him safely—and far—behind.

Her wolf howled piteously in her mind, but she jerked herself out of the sadness and straightened. It was the right thing to do. She would respect and protect her mate by leaving him behind and taking her problems far, far away.

She leaned away, and he released his tight hold on her and stroked the stray tears from her cheeks with his thumbs. Their eyes met and held, and in that moment, she knew that walking away from Bo Elliott was going to be the most difficult thing she'd ever done in her life.

But she would do it.

For him.

Chapter Four

Bo stood a few feet away from Reika as she called her mother and told her what had happened. He had never heard of the Were-Animal Alliance, and he made a mental note to speak to Jason about it. If there was a group that was helping wolves like Reika escape dangerous situations, than their pack would want to get in on it.

He'd never had a woman cry in his arms like that before. It had broken something inside him to see her so completely torn up. He had a feeling that a lot of the tears she cried were ones she'd been holding in for a long time. She struck him as the sort of woman who didn't burden others with her pain, the sort who would smile in public and weep in private. He was humbled that she felt comfortable enough with him already to let go like that.

Because she's my mate.

He shook the thought away as quickly as it entered his mind. He knew she was his, but he wasn't so damn selfish as to tie her to a broken creature like himself. It would kill him, but he would set her free and then watch her walk away.

A knock on the front door pulled Bo's mind away from his morose thoughts, as Reika spoke in low tones to her parents. He admired her for trying to get away and doing so without involving her family. He'd get her back to them safely, but not before he put those lynxes down for good.

Teller stood at the door. The ebony-skinned wolf was the best tracker in the pack, orphaned at a young age and adopted by a childless, mated pair in the Tressel Pack. He was younger than Bo by a few years but was a good friend and an even better wolf to have at his back.

Bo let Teller in. "They're skulking around, three lynx males. Let me tell you, man, cats reek." Teller made a face, and Bo laughed.

"Have they come into Allen?" Bo offered Teller some coffee, but he declined.

"Yes, last night. A pickup truck with out-of-state plates was seen driving slowly through town. Jason alerted Trick to keep an eye out for strange things, and Trick called him last night. Logan and I went out looking for them, but the truck was gone by then. We shifted and ran the perimeter of town. I caught the scent of two of the males over by the trailer park, but it was several hours old."

Patrick Flannigan, aka Trick, was Allen's chief of police, human, and married to a she-wolf in the Tressel Pack.

"So the lynxes hunted for her in their form and then came back with their truck to sweep through town?" Bo asked, rubbing his chin in thought.

Reika, having ended the call, joined him and Teller. Her voice was soft, filled with worry. "No, they tracked you, Bo. The trail of my scent would have ended when you put me in your truck. But your scent is probably all over this town." She wrung her hands in worry. "I should go. Keep moving, or call the WAA and ask them to help me disappear."

So that was her plan? Hell no. Bo's wolf growled angrily. "You don't have anything to worry about, Reika. I told you that you would be safe here with me, and I meant it."

Teller introduced himself to Reika and then asked Bo to step outside. Once they were standing on the snow dusted front porch, Teller said, "It's not going to take those lynxes long to find you. All they'd have to do is break into Pete's garage and search the files for your address, or ask one of the humans around town where you live. The humans in this town wouldn't think twice about helping out a stranger, damn southern hospitality and all."

"I'm not letting her run off on her own, T."

"I didn't say you should, Bo. I get what's going on here. I'm just saying that you need to be smart. Jason wants you to bring Reika over this afternoon so that Cades can meet her and the upper ranked can figure out what to do."

Nodding, Bo shook Teller's hand and watched his friend get in his car and drive off. As a tracker, Teller wasn't really ranked within the pack. He was a unique entity, under the rule of the alpha, but not part of the ranking system. A talented tracker was worth his weight in gold, and no alpha in his right mind would put a tracker in the ranking and allow him to fight for his place. If a tracker was injured, he couldn't track. Teller was highly regarded in the pack, a good man to know and a wolf who could find anyone, anywhere.

Bo walked back inside. Reika was sitting on the couch, his cell still in her hand. He had been able to overhear the majority of her conversation with her parents. They had been frantic when she disappeared, especially when the leader of the lynx told them that his grandsons, the three males who had hurt her, were already on their way to bring her home.

The whole situation was rotten and worse than he'd imagined. He didn't fault her alpha for what had happened. He'd sacrificed one wolf for his pack, and after knowing Jason his whole life and seeing what he dealt with on a regular basis as leader, sometimes the good of the many really did outweigh the needs of the few. Or the one sweet she-wolf who was trembling on his couch as she tried to keep it together. He could taste her fear like a bitter pill on the back of his tongue.

Something she said had stuck in his mind. "You mentioned them breeding on you."

"Yeah?" She looked up at him, her blue eyes luminous and sad.

"It sounds like there's more to it than just creating the next generation of lynxes. What is it?"

She pursed her lush lips together and then sighed, rubbing at a spot between her eyes with her thumb. "I'm an apex."

"I don't know that word." He joined her on the couch.

"A healer. In my family, all the females are healers. My family is rumored to be one of the oldest family lines in the history of wolf-kind, maybe even as far back as the first wolf, depending on the lore you read. I'm a blue-coat. You'll only see my coloring in my family line. Not only is my coloring unique to my family, but the females are magically powerful. Not physically, necessarily, but powerful with old magic. Healing magic." She glanced at his leg before speaking. "The lynx king sensed what I was, even at seven, and decided to take me instead of the money to replace his horse. It was either promise me to the three lynxes or watch Ben die at that point. My parents, my alpha, they made the right choice."

"Reika …" he started, but she cut him off by picking up his cell and opening a blank text message.

"Who are you texting?" He had a sneaking suspicion he knew the answer.

"The WAA. I hope they'll be able to get me out of here fast and that they won't hold me responsible for what happened to the two wolves who came to help me." He snatched the phone from her fingers. "Hey!"

"No way, Reika. If you think I'm going to just let you disappear with those lynxes able to scent you out, you're out of your ever-loving mind. What I will do is figure out how to break the promise that was made on your behalf and send them packing. Once you're safe from them, you can go back to your family. In the meantime, you're staying put." He adjusted the settings on his cell and locked it so it required a password. He glanced up from his cell, and she glared at him. He was sure that she knew exactly what he'd just done to his phone.

"I don't want anyone to get hurt because of me, Bo. If I stay here, I'll bring them into your town. Innocent people could get hurt. *Will* get hurt," she insisted.

"You're not going anywhere. Teller is going to go find your rental car so it can be returned to the company and your bag can be brought here."

"How will he find it? I have no idea what town I was in, or the name of the park, or even how long I was running."

"Teller's our pack tracker. He's going to follow your scent. Don't worry about it, okay? I've got this, sweetheart. All you need to do is just trust me. Can you do that?"

He really hoped she would say yes. He'd never cared if a woman trusted him or not, but it was seriously important now. If she took off because she didn't trust him to keep her safe, if she got hurt because of it, he'd lose his mind.

"Okay, Bo," she said after a long moment. "I trust you."

He could see her mind working. Even though she said that she would trust him, she was trying to figure out how to get away from him and get out on her own. He applauded her desire to keep others safe and keep the burden on herself, but he wasn't about to let her waltz into hell alone.

She was his mate. He knew that with more certainty now than he had as he'd watched her recover in her sleep. His wolf rumbled an agreement. No female had ever made him feel the way that she did. He knew he was broken, and not worthy of someone as incredible as her, especially with such a powerful family line behind her. But he could still make sure she was safe. He had no choice. Even though his wolf rebelled at the thought of letting her go, she deserved a mate who could protect her for the rest of their lives, wolf and man, not one who would be crippled within a few years. He would set her free from the lynxes, and then let her go. It was the right thing to do.

That afternoon, he drove them to Jason and Cades' home. Reika had been quiet for most of the morning, only speaking when he spoke to her first. As he watched her look around while they walked up the front porch of their home, he could sense her wariness. She was looking for the lynxes.

"A handful of our best fighters are patrolling the grounds, sweetheart, so you're safe here." Bo held his hand out to her. He waited for her to take it, watching as she took one last look around and then relaxed, but only fractionally.

"I've upset your entire pack. It's not right."

He felt the warm weight of her hand. "Of course it's right. Not only are you a wolf and our kind, but you're—" he faltered. He wasn't going to put the word *mate* out there. She was freaked out enough as it was. Thinking quickly, he opened the front door and pulled her inside. "You're allowed to choose who you mate with and what you will and won't do with your life."

Her lips parted slightly, and her head cocked to the side. He wanted so badly to pull her into his arms and kiss her. Feel her lush body pressed against him. Watch her fall apart in ecstasy.

She doesn't need your baggage, his mocking inner voice said.

Shut up, his wolf growled in warning.

Reika followed him into the kitchen, where Jason and Cades stood at the counter. Michael, Jason's brother and pack second, was seated at the kitchen table, along with Linus, fourth and Logan, fifth ranked. Bo's wolf bristled at Logan, who was the only unmated male around. Bo struggled with his desire to push Reika behind him, to shield her from Logan's eyes. A possessive wolf was the last thing she needed, when the lynxes had nothing *but* possession on their minds.

Cades and Jason came over, and Jason introduced her and the others at the table. Bo sat Reika down between himself and Cades as the two joined the group. He kept his hand on the back of Reika's chair, laying silent claim to her.

While they discussed the situation with the lynx males, Bo's mind drifted constantly to Reika. Her sweet, natural scent was like a beacon for him. He found himself unconsciously leaning towards her, wanting to stroke her soft skin, kiss her full lips. It was going to be hard to keep away from her. Reminding himself that the last thing she needed was his sorry ass panting after her, he curled his fingers into the wood of the chair back and focused on the conversation.

Jason's dad, Peter, walked into the kitchen, head down, reading a large, leather-covered volume of pack law. "Right." He put the book down on the table, the yellowed pages filled with writing in the old language. "A blood-debt can only be called by one powerful enough to break it."

"Blood-debt?" Cades asked.

Peter lifted his head. "Yes. They sealed the promise with blood, didn't they, Reika? Yours and the three males?"

She shivered and nodded, embarrassment flushing her cheeks. Fuck it. Bo put his arm around her and drew her against him. She stiffened only slightly, and then relaxed. She rubbed the tip of the ring finger on her right hand. He wondered if they had taken the blood from there. The thought of someone cutting her, drawing her blood when she was a child, made his hackles rise. The sorts of people who marked children and promised them to rapists to become brood mares weren't the sorts of shifters he wanted to get to know. The sooner they were out of Reika's life, the better.

"One powerful enough to break it. What does that mean?" Jason asked. "It's not a physical bond. They're not mated."

Peter looked at Reika for a long moment, and she shook her head ever so slightly. He made a small humming sound in his throat and turned his attention back to the book. *What the hell?*

She fidgeted in her chair and moved his arm off her shoulder as she stood. Her voice was calm and even, but her pretty blue eyes were filled with dread. "Can someone show me where the bathroom is?"

"Sure, this way." Cades stood and took her to the half bath on the first floor. He watched her go, her movements stiff and anxious.

When the door shut, Teller said, "Anyone else think that the only person who can break the blood-debt is her truemate?"

Peter nodded. "It's pretty clear here in the old texts. The blood-debt was used as a promise between packs in the old days. When packs made peace, they often arranged marriages between the alphas' children, sealing the promise with blood. The only thing that could break the promise was if either of the children found their truemates before the mating occurred. The truemates would fight to break the blood-debt. If they were successful, then the debt was erased. If they lost, however, they were not allowed to claim their mates."

Jason leaned back in his chair. "I looked up her pack. They're not much bigger than us, settled in Columbus. The alpha is old-school, not as much as Karly's family, but honorable."

"It's barbaric," Cades groused, bringing her baby, Lyric, into the room. The five month-old baby girl hung onto her mother with her fists tightened in Cades' hair. "She was a child. They never should have agreed to it."

"I don't think they had a choice, Cadence," Peter said.

"Bullshit," Cades growled. "There is *always* a choice. And you can be damn sure if someone tried to bind Riki to three males in the name of honor, they'd do it over my dead body."

Bo was sure that would be the exact scenario. Bo felt that same protective need sweep over him with Reika. He might not be worthy of her, but she deserved more than males who would force her and make her submit, and hurt her the way they did.

Speaking of Reika ...

He glanced towards the bathroom with a sinking feeling. Without even bothering to go to the bathroom, he walked from the kitchen, out the back door, and moved around the side of the house. He saw the bathroom window open, and the spot where she had landed when she slipped from inside.

Her footsteps were easy enough to follow in the snow, but she hadn't gone far. She stood a few hundred yards into the woods, her back against a tree, a cell phone in her hand.

"Going somewhere, sweetheart?" He stopped in front of her and put his hands on his hips. He was both furious and turned on. She shouldn't have tried to walk away, but she was damn sneaky, and help him, he liked that.

She chucked the phone at him and folded her arms over her chest. "You people sure are trusting."

He caught it, glancing down and finding Cades' bright pink cell phone, with a password preventing it from being used. He tried not to laugh, but he couldn't help it. While Reika glared at him, he laughed harder. It was damn funny.

When he had laughed his fill, he tucked the phone into his back pocket and stepped close to her. "You said you trusted me."

She tried to look away, but he caught her chin and made her look at him. Her eyes said it all. She was feeling the mate-pull as much as him.

"I do. I just don't want anyone else to get hurt."

"I'll break their tie to you, Reika. You'll be free to mate with who you want."

"No!" she shouted, her hands suddenly gripping his arms. "You can't. It's too dangerous. They're crazy and relentless. They'll never give up on having me."

He let his beast free enough for his canines to elongate, and he scratched the inside of his palm, drawing blood. Pressing his hand to her neck, he said, "I swear on my life, Reika Snow, that I will see you free of your blood-debt to the lynx clan."

Her chest rose and fell as she breathed, almost panting, her fingers tightening on his arms.

"Why?" Her voice came out raw.

"So you can go home to your family and live your life the way you want." It would kill him, but he'd see her safe so she could have a normal life.

Her brow furrowed, her mouth drawing down into a frown. "Go home?"

"Yes. Back to your family. Let me set you free, sweetheart."

Her eyes dropped down to his mouth, and her pulse sped. His body sprang to life, heating with need and desire. "Bo," she said quietly, her voice just a bare whisper.

He fell on her, leaning into her body, as their mouths crashed together. He pushed his tongue past her lips and drank in the heady taste of her, heat and woman and sweetness all rolled into one. He tilted his head and slipped his hand around to her neck, kneading the flesh just under her thick hair. He danced his tongue against hers and ate the throaty moans she made like they were food he could live on. She trembled, and the human part of him remembered that it was damn cold outside and neither of them wore coats. The wolf side of him, however, wanted to tear her clothes off and claim her, despite the cold.

She flattened her hand against his chest and pressed, and he allowed himself to be pushed away. Her eyes were bright, her mouth swollen from the amazing kiss, and her breasts heaving as she panted for breath.

"We should get back," she said.

"Yeah." He almost apologized. But the truth was he didn't regret kissing her. Of course it would make it just that much harder for him to let her go, now that he'd had a taste of her and held her close. A twinge in his leg brought him out of sappy romance-land and into cruel reality.

"It'll be okay, Reika," he said as he put his arm around her and walked her back to the house. They stayed for dinner with Jason and Cades. Michael and his wife, Shyne, joined them. Although Reika was friendly and talked to the women, Bo could feel the tension in her. She was going to keep trying to get away from him, and he had a feeling that it wasn't only because she didn't want innocents hurt for her, but also because she didn't want *him* to be hurt.

That night, he watched her walk into the bedroom and shut the door. She had promised, several times, that she wouldn't try to leave overnight. He didn't trust her a damn bit because she looked like a doe about to bolt, but he had to show her good faith. He settled on the couch, shoes and shirt off, jeans on. He never slept well on the couch, although he never really slept well anywhere.

Reika had been kind enough not to ask about his leg, but he was aware that she had glanced at it several times during the day. He wasn't really ready to flay open his soul and share the story. Because sharing the story meant showing the leg, and he didn't think he could bear to see the disgust roll through her when she saw the mangled flesh of his leg.

The irrational, primal part of him argued that she was his mate, and she would love him no matter what. But the rational part of him that had spent so many years watching doctors and nurses startle when they saw his leg, and then the pity that followed, didn't think he could handle seeing that in her eyes.

He lay in the darkness, staring at the ceiling, waiting for sleep to come. He hoped to hell he didn't have a nightmare. It had been embarrassing waking up from his nightmare to find her worried about him. Not to mention how weak he must appear.

He was so deep in thought he wasn't aware that Reika was in the room with him until she curled up next to him, tucking herself against him in the deep couch. His arms immediately went around her as she snuggled against him.

"Sweetheart?"

"I'm cold," she said.

He pulled the afghan from the back of the couch and draped it over her. She didn't feel cold; she felt flushed. And she smelled aroused.

His cock reacted, hardening and scraping against his zipper. He muffled the groan in his throat. "I can kick up the heat. It's not comfortable here on the couch."

She looked up at him. "Only if you come with me."

Well, he didn't think that was a good idea. If he took her to bed, he wouldn't be able to keep his hands off her, so it was best to stay on the couch. As it was, his body was screaming to roll on top of her and find out if she was as hot and wet as she smelled.

"Goodnight, Reika."

"Night, Bo."

When morning came and Bo woke, he realized that he'd actually had a good night's sleep for the first time in many years. Reika was like a balm for his body. The constant twinge of pain was there, but it had dulled enough so he could sleep. Amazed, he lay with her while she slept, wishing he could bottle the feeling.

Just thinking about letting her go made his wolf prowl in his mind, snarling and unhappy. But it was for the best, Bo knew. She might have some healing abilities, but she hadn't offered to heal him, which told him that he was truly beyond hope. No doctors or specialists had ever been able to help him with the constant pain and nothing that his aunt Lia had ever made for him with her herbal skills had ever worked beyond a temporary numbing that seemed to make the pain more intense when the herbs faded.

Extracting himself from the couch without waking Reika, he showered and changed for work. Although the last thing he wanted to do was leave her, he did have a job to do. And Cades and Karly were coming to spend the day with Reika, and two of the younger males were going to hang around outside and keep an eye on the house.

Reika was sitting on the bed when he came out of the bathroom after brushing his teeth. She smiled at him as they passed when she walked into the bathroom. He finished getting ready for work and walked into the kitchen. Reika had brewed a pot of coffee and fixed a cup for him. He'd never had anyone make a cup of coffee for him. Then again, he hadn't ever had a woman spend the entire night at his house, either.

Reika joined him in the kitchen twenty minutes later. She had changed into the other outfit that Cadence had brought for her, a thick sweater and a pair of dark jeans. Her hair was damp.

"After work today, I'll take you to a mall, and you can pick out some things of your own, okay?"

She looked surprised. "You don't have to do that."

"Why wouldn't I? Cades' clothes don't quite fit you right, and you said you only had two changes of clothes in the bag you packed, which isn't enough. We'll grab a bite to eat while we're out. Unless you want toaster waffles for dinner."

She chuckled and shook her head. "I don't know when I'll be able to pay you back, Bo."

He cupped her face with one hand and stroked her cheek. "Don't give it a second thought, sweetheart."

Memories of the kiss they'd shared in the woods the day before flashed through his mind, and he found himself leaning into her, wanting to taste her and kiss her … devour her.

A knock on the door threw cold water on them, and he stepped back quickly, reminding himself that he wasn't planning for her to stick around once he freed her from the lynxes. He walked to the front door, cursing inwardly at his erection and at his wolf's insistence that they couldn't allow her to leave, even after she was freed. He opened the door.

Karly and Cades stood on the front porch, cheeks bright from the cold air and smiles on their faces.

"Come on in, ladies." Bo stepped back and held the door open as Cades and Karly walked inside. Karly held a plastic container in her hands. As Bo shut the door, he nodded at the wolf standing in the front yard, knowing that the other one was in the backyard, already watching for trouble. He didn't like leaving her at all, but knowing she had people watching over her helped to ease some of that burden.

As he expected, when Reika saw Karly and Cades, she bristled with anger.

Pulling him aside as Karly lifted the lid from the plastic container and Cades looked in the cupboards for dishes, Reika hissed, "I do *not* need babysitters."

She was so fierce and passionate, and he wanted to silence her protests with kisses and nibbles.

Not the time.

"Baby, first of all, I have no idea if the lynxes know where you are or not. I would never take the chance of leaving you on your own while I go to work. If I could stay home with you I would, but I have a deadline and a customer waiting. You're just going to have to suck it up."

Her mouth dropped open. "Did you just tell me to suck it up?"

"Yeah." He grinned and tweaked her chin. "I swore on my wolf's blood that I would see you safe and that means I'm in charge of what happens until that comes to pass. Suck. It. Up."

She let out a small gasp of surprise and her eyes widened, and then she snapped her teeth together. He imagined she was thinking about taking a bite out of him. At least she stopped arguing.

He kissed her cheek, snagged a fresh cinnamon roll, and grabbed his coat. Casting a glance backwards, he saw Reika plaster a smile on her face and greet Karly and Cades with enthusiasm. He knew she wasn't happy, but she managed to convey that she was, regardless. Once more he realized just how long she'd been perfecting the facade of being happy when she wasn't, and it strengthened his resolve to see her free and safe. No matter what, he would put down those lynxes and give her back her life.

Chapter Five

When the door shut behind Bo as he headed off to work, Reika looked at Cades and Karly with a smile so broad that her cheeks hurt. She had lots of practice putting on a happy face so no one knew how bad she felt inside.

Cades, female alpha and hybrid wolf, looked at Reika with an arched brow and said, "You don't have to pretend to be happy to see us, but just know that Bo has the best intentions. You're important to him, and like any male of worth, he's going to make sure you're safe even if he has to trust others to keep you so."

She opened her mouth to retort that Bo had no idea what he was getting himself into by putting his pack on the line to help her, but she could tell from the fierce look in Cades' eyes that nothing Reika could say would make her leave the house. She'd seen a young man standing out in the front yard, and she had a feeling he wasn't the only one around, which meant taking off—even if she could find a way to ditch the two women—wasn't going to happen.

Face it ... you're stuck.

She sighed audibly and let her unnatural smile drop. "I appreciate you both being here."

Karly gestured to the small kitchen table, and Reika sat down. Karly, with long black hair and delicate features, used tongs to place a thick cinnamon roll on a plate in front of Reika while Cades poured a mug of coffee and set it in front of her. Karly said, "I'm trying out a new recipe for these rolls, so tell me what you think."

Karly and Cades joined her at the table, and Reika picked up the glazed treat and took a bite. She was unable to stifle the happy hum as the delicious flavors of cinnamon and brown sugar exploded on her tongue.

Ben would love to have this recipe.

"It's so good, Karly. You're very talented," Reika said, putting the roll down and fixing her coffee with cream and sugar.

Karly smiled brightly, and both she and Cades took bites of theirs, and for several moments, there were only pleased murmurs and happy hums as the three of them ate their rolls.

Karly picked up her coffee mug and took a sip. "Bo said you're from Columbus. Is your home pack very big?"

"Just a little bigger than yours, from what he told me. My family is small, just my parents and my younger brother, Ben."

There was a bit of silence, and then Reika added, "It's not that I don't appreciate what Bo's trying to do for me, but I don't want anyone else to get hurt. It's bad enough that the two wolves from the WAA were injured trying to help me. I don't want to add to the blood on my hands."

Cades reached over and put her hand over Reika's. Even though Cades wasn't a true wolf and didn't shift, Reika could feel her power as alpha. "There is no blood on your hands, Reika. The wolves who were hurt, that's on the lynxes, not you. And it's not just Bo who wants to see you safe. It's all of us. It's awful what happened to you, what you've suffered knowing they were waiting for you, and we're not about to let you go off on your own. Bo found you when you needed a champion, and his pack supports you one hundred percent."

The sincerity in Cades' words touched Reika deeply. She placed her other hand on top of Cades' and said, "Thank you."

It would be harder to leave Bo behind, now that he'd gotten his pack involved, but she was even more certain that she had no choice. He was a male of worth, a wolf of honor, and he deserved to live a long, full life and find happiness, not shoulder her burden and die for her. She just couldn't let that happen.

As they finished their breakfast, Reika found out that both women had children; Karly's son, Remy, was almost a year old, and Cades' daughter, Lyric, was five months old. The women had seemed to enjoy having a day off while their children were watched by their mutual grandparents. The three sat on the couch in the front room and watched daytime TV. They talked about everything except the lynxes and her blood-debt, for which she was grateful. It was easy to relax around Cades and Karly, who had funny stories to share about the pack members, including Bo. Cades had grown up with Bo, who was a few years older than her, and remembered him as the dark, brooding guy who was quick to stand up for his friends and never backed down from a fight. Apparently, he hadn't changed much since high school.

Wistfully, Reika felt like she could be friends with both of them, if she were sticking around. They were just the sort of girls she liked hanging around with. She didn't have many friends in her home pack because her future loomed like a shadow over her. As it grew closer to her time to be taken away, the friends she did have drifted away, as if they were afraid to be sucked into the lynx clan just by being her friend. She didn't fault them for wanting to protect themselves, but she'd been lonely.

It was almost five when Bo's truck pulled into the driveway in front of the house, followed by a large black SUV.

Bo got out of his truck, rubbing at his right leg before he moved up the front walk. Once more, she wondered about the extent of his injuries. The doors to the SUV opened, and Reika recognized Michael and his wife, Shyne, as they got out and followed Bo into the house.

Bo smiled at Reika when he opened the door, taking off his jacket and hanging it on a hook next to the door. "Hi, sweetheart! You remember Michael and Shyne."

"Nice to see you again," Reika said and smiled at them.

"You, too, Reika." Shyne smiled easily and then moved to talk to Cades and Karly who were putting on their coats.

"Did you have a nice day?" Bo asked.

A very small part of her wanted to be bratty and tell him that, in fact, she didn't have a good day under the watchful gaze of an alpha female and an angel mate. But looking into his rich, hazel eyes and seeing the earnestness there, she couldn't say it.

"I did. Cades told me a bunch of stories from when you were younger."

His smile faltered, and he cast his narrowed eyes towards Cades, who pulled on her jacket, smiling innocently. "I don't know what she's talking about, Bo."

He grunted under his breath and thanked Karly and Cades for hanging out with her for the day. As Reika said goodbye to them as well, Bo shut the door and turned to her. "Michael and Shyne are going to join us for dinner. There's a strip mall not too far from here. It has a few clothing stores in it and some restaurants nearby."

He left her in the front room with Michael and Shyne so he could take a quick shower and change. Michael plopped down on the couch with a yawn, and Shyne smiled fondly at him as she came to stand next to Reika.

"I wanted to see if you'd like to come hang out at the community center with me tomorrow. I teach some fitness classes for the older wolves who live in the development where the center is, and the staff could always use a hand in the office."

Reika didn't know what to say. Shyne seemed like a sweet woman, and she didn't want to insult her, especially since she could guess that Bo had put her up to it.

As if sensing her hesitancy, Shyne smiled softly. "When I first met Michael, I had a few were-hyenas who were interested in me, and they really came on strong and freaked me out. I stayed with Michael after that, but the first few days when I was alone in the house without anyone to talk to while he worked made me batty. I know it's not the same situation, and I don't mean to belittle what you're going through, but it'll be fun to hang out and get to know each other. The wolves in the retirement development are so fun, and someone always offers to make lunch for me. I know you'll be welcome."

When Shyne was being so kind, Reika couldn't say no. "Sounds good. What time?"

"I'll pick you up about nine, and just dress in jeans or whatever. I don't expect you to workout or anything, unless you want to."

Reika made a face, and Shyne chuckled. Shyne had Hispanic-skin, jet black hair and warm, brown eyes, and even though she wore jeans and a thick sweater, Reika could tell she was fit.

Bo walked out of the bedroom wearing faded jeans and a long sleeved, button down shirt. His dark hair was slightly damp, and he had a jaw full of stubble that she imagined would abrade her skin just right when they kissed ... when they touched ... when he slid down her body and rubbed against her thighs.

Oh, shit.

Her whole body heated at the wicked thoughts she couldn't seem to get a handle on, and she met Bo's eyes as he came to her and reached for his jacket. She saw the lust that flared in his eyes as he drew in a slow breath. He was so close that she could have kissed him, she could have touched that stubble with her fingertips, but instead she took a big step backwards and forced herself to think about unsexy things like ...

Drawing a blank on anything unsexy, she fisted her hands at her sides and clenched her teeth together. Bo seemed frozen in place for several seconds, and then he grabbed his jacket off the hook and held it out to her. "We'll get you a coat when we go out, sweetheart. You can use mine for now."

Before she could ask what he was going to wear, he moved a hooded sweatshirt from another hook and pulled another jacket from underneath. She slipped the too-big leather coat on and was surrounded immediately by the delicious scent of him. It was going to be a long night.

Shyne offered the passenger seat to Bo so she could join Reika in the second row, and Bo accepted. Michael and Bo talked about a car Bo was restoring, and Shyne discussed a movie she and Michael had seen the previous weekend. Reika liked Shyne and found her witty humor and easy smile infectious. By the time Michael parked in front of a store called Mona's, she'd let go of all her worries concerning the lynxes and decided to just enjoy herself.

"Alright, we'll be here when you're done," Michael said as he turned and winked at them.

"No way, baby, you're not getting off that easy." Shyne laughed. "Get your cute ass out of the car and hold my purse when I go try things on."

Michael made a face at her, but Reika could see the affection flashing in his eyes. "Thanks for complimenting my ass, love, but no."

Shyne leaned forward slightly and brushed her fingers across his cheek. "You remember the sexy little black number I bought for Christmas as a surprise?"

Michael's brows rose, and he grinned. "Oh, yeah."

Shyne sat back with a wicked, triumphant smirk and said, "If you ever want to see it again, you'll move. Now."

Michael stared at her in shock, and then barked out a laugh. "Got me there. Alright, alright."

Michael got out of the truck and jogged around to Shyne's side so he could open her door. Bo got out and walked around the front of the SUV towards Reika. Shyne winked at Reika and chuckled. "Men."

Bo opened Reika's door and held his hand out to her. "They're funny," she said to him, as she squeezed his hand tighter so she didn't slip on the still icy parking lot.

"I'm glad you think so. Michael's the smartass of the group, in case you didn't realize."

"I picked up on it."

Mona's was a boutique store owned by a rogue wolf—Mona herself—who greeted them when they walked in the front door as if they were old friends. After a quick up-and-down look, the older woman took Shyne and Reika by the hands and pulled them into the clothes racks, calling over her shoulder for Bo and Michael to have a seat.

An hour later, Bo was paying for several pairs of jeans, sweaters, underclothes, a winter jacket, and two pairs of shoes. Michael was cuddling Shyne as she sat on his lap and thanked him for buying her a new sweater.

"I'll pay you back, Bo, I promise," Reika said as Mona handed her two bags with her clothes inside.

Bo took the bags from her hands and gathered them both in one hand. He placed his hand on her elbow and ushered her towards the door. "I didn't ask you to, Reika. I promised I would take care of you, and part of that is making sure you don't freeze to death with no clothes or starve to death without food."

Michael opened the back of the SUV, and they stowed the bags. As Bo held open her door for her, she looked up at him and said, "My protests aren't making a difference, are they?"

He smiled. "Not really."

"I'm not going to stop protesting."

"I'm not going to *start* listening," he countered.

She chuckled and lifted onto her toes and kissed him once, softly, before climbing into the SUV. "Thank you."

He nodded and shut the door.

They ate at one of those fifties-style burger places, and Michael and Shyne kept the conversation light and funny, talking about the pack and the small town of Allen.

When they said goodbye to Michael and Shyne once they were back at Bo's house, Bo shut the door and locked it. He hung their jackets.

"You asked them to go with us so that we could go in Michael's SUV and have less chance of the lynxes finding us while we were out?" She looked up at him.

He nodded. "That's one reason, and also that I knew you'd like Shyne, and Michael is one of my closest friends. Did you have fun?"

"I did. It was nice to not really think about anything serious for a change."

"Then my mission was a success." He tucked a lock of hair behind her ear and smiled.

She took in a slow breath and the scent of him, dark and spicy, a combination of his cologne and the wolf underneath, washed over her. *Her mate.*

It would have been so easy to fall into his arms and tell him how to break the blood-debt, ask him to fight for her because they were mates and she wanted him, but she fought against the urge. With another whispered *thanks*, she took her new things into the bedroom and put them away. After cleaning up, she changed into one of his T-shirts and settled into bed.

It was cold and empty, and after awhile, she did what she had done the night before and walked into the family room and cuddled against him. It was the second best night's sleep she'd ever had.

"So it's pretty simple," Susan, human mate of a werewolf and the woman who ran the community center, said as Reika sat in a chair behind a metal desk. "Enter in the information for the flyer, make it look pretty, and then print out fifty copies. Then when you're done with that, you can print out address labels, and we'll run them around to the houses after lunch. Sound good?"

Reika had worked in the Dean's office of the community college she went to for her office management degree. She hadn't really expected to go to college, but her parents wanted to give her every opportunity to meet other wolves. So she was very familiar with the tasks she'd been given, and it would be no trouble at all.

"I'll get right on it."

"Good." Susan squeezed her shoulder. "You're a lifesaver. I've got so much to do. Hey, maybe if you finish up early, you can start working on the monthly newsletter."

"Sure, Susan, whatever you need. I'm here as long as Shyne is."

Susan clapped her hands happily and then set to work at her own desk across the room. Reika heard upbeat music suddenly and knew that Shyne had started her exercise class. The retirement development was for wolves who were part of the Tressel Pack but didn't want to participate in the rankings, had stepped down from their rankings due to injury or age, or were the human mates of wolves who had died. The development had several dozen homes, the community center, and 24-hour security in the form of a revolving tour of pack members.

Shyne had picked her up promptly at nine, and Reika had noticed a car pull away from the curb in front of Bo's home and follow them. When she asked, Shyne said that it was a wolf from the retirement development who Michael and Bo asked to follow the two women during the day to make sure they weren't followed and to keep an eye out for trouble.

The day passed quickly. Shyne appeared at lunchtime and told her they were going to lunch with one of the she-wolves from her class, and Reika spent an hour in a homey kitchen enjoying the most delicious chicken and dumplings she'd ever had. After lunch, Reika and Susan walked around the development and handed out flyers, and then Reika worked on the monthly newsletter until Shyne finished for the day.

Susan hugged Reika tightly. "I could use you here, Reika. Part-time, a few days a week?"

Reika felt the blood drain from her face. "Susan, I—" She didn't know what to say.

Susan glanced at Shyne, who subtly shook her head. Susan smiled breezily and said, "Just think about it. Take your time and let me know. Thank you so much for your help today, Reika."

Reika smiled tightly and said goodbye, leaving with Shyne.

When she pulled in front of Bo's home, Shyne put her hand on Reika's arm and stopped her from opening the car door. "It wouldn't be so bad to live here, would it? Bo's pretty awesome. Michael speaks so highly of him and how much he suffered with his injury and everything. And the pack is so cool. I'm not even a wolf, and they treat me like I've lived here my whole life. Of course, that might be because Michael would kick ass if someone didn't treat me right, but I'd like to think it's because I'm so charming and sweet."

Reika chuckled at Shyne's attempt at humor. "You are sweet, Shyne. My life is really complicated."

"*Life* is complicated. I lost my parents before I learned how to read, and then the woman who took me in died when I was twelve, and I spent six years in a group foster home before I had to leave at eighteen. I know all about how complicated and difficult life can be. Granted, I wasn't arranged to be married when I was in elementary school, but I do know how valuable a good man is, and how rare real love is. You're scared, I get that. But don't give up on finding real love because of fear. Just my two cents."

Reika opened her mouth to tell Shyne that she really didn't know what she was talking about. It wasn't that Reika was afraid to love Bo because a part of her was already half in love with him anyway. She was afraid to give into that love because he was the kind of guy who would go off to fight for her and might die. And she was definitely afraid of that. Instead, though, because she didn't want to hurt Shyne's feelings and she genuinely liked her, Reika patted Shyne's hand and said, "I appreciate you spending time with me today, Shyne, and I'll consider all you said."

"Good." Shyne nodded her head as Reika got out of the car and shut the door. Reika waved at the car waiting behind Shyne's car, and the wolf behind the wheel waved back as he reversed down the driveway and waited for Shyne to back down as well, and then they both left. Reika stood on the front porch for a while, until the cold nipped at her and forced her inside.

As she hung up her coat, she turned to Bo and said, "Who is babysitting me tomorrow?"

He chuckled. "I thought you'd like to go hang out with Karly at her restaurant. They're getting ready to open in a couple of weeks, and she and a bunch of wolves are getting it ready."

She walked over to him until they were just inches apart. "How long are you going to keep this up?"

"As long as I have to in order to know that you're safe."

"I'll never be safe, Bo. You're just delaying the inevitable and potentially causing innocent people to get hurt."

He growled, low and threatening, and she shrugged and turned away. "I'm just being honest."

She walked to the bedroom to take a shower before dinner, but she still heard him say, "So am I."

Chapter Six

Logan

Thursday morning, Logan Jackson smiled gratefully at Karly as she handed him a cup of coffee. Bo had called him the night before and asked if he would hang out at the restaurant for the day while his "friend" Reika was there, to make sure nothing happened.

Logan had never met a lynx before, but he knew something about them and their strange ways. Never putting down roots and traveling constantly seemed like a hard life. Maybe that was why they were such dicks. Although Bo wouldn't say it outright, Logan knew from talking to Michael and Jason that Reika was Bo's truemate. Bo had some pretty serious self-esteem issues thanks to his bum leg, but Logan didn't think there was anything lacking in him. He was a good friend, a fierce wolf, and a good man to have at his back in a fight. Logan was happy to watch over the she-wolf for his friend.

Karly was hoping to open the restaurant in time for Valentine's Day, which was just a couple of weeks away, and Logan was looking forward to having a chance to eat her delicious food more often. She always cooked on the full moons and for the monthly high-ranked pack meetings that he attended as fifth in rank, but to be able to just wander in for lunch or dinner whenever he wanted was a great benefit to having her open up her own restaurant.

Peter Gerrick, who had been alpha before Jason took over, walked in from the back of the restaurant with Reika, who smiled even though her eyes were screaming she was not a happy camper. Bo was keeping her under careful watch while he was at work—not only for her own safety, but also because he was worried she was going to try to take off the moment he left her alone. Logan agreed with Bo's tactic. If Logan had found his own truemate and she was in danger and trying to escape to keep him out of harm's way, he would do anything in his power to make sure she stayed safe and close, even if he had to trust others to help.

Nodding at Peter as he left, Logan said good morning to Reika, who smiled sweetly, but not sincerely, and joined Karly at a server station. A handful of young wolves worked diligently at cleaning in the dining room. When Karly decided to open the closed restaurant after the previous owners left town, the decision had involved a lot of work to update the furniture and decor. Now the restaurant was being cleaned from floor to ceiling, fixtures and windows were being polished, walls were being washed, and carpeting was being steam cleaned. The kitchen was being scrubbed, and the small office had been completely redone to make a comfortable space for Karly to work out her mouth-watering menus.

"Logan? I have chocolate croissants and blueberry scones in the kitchen. Help yourself, and don't forget to tell me what you think." Karly looked over her shoulder and smiled at him, and then turned back to Reika.

"You know I'll love them. I love everything you make." He chuckled.

"Still, a girl likes to be reassured." Karly laughed.

He heard Karly explain to Reika that she needed her to proofread the new menus and inserts that detailed daily specials and Reika promising to check the information carefully. Logan had heard that Susan, who worked at the community center, loved Reika so much that she had been singing her praises to the pack and had even offered her a part-time job.

Logan walked into the kitchen and found two trays, choosing a chocolate-filled croissant and taking a quick bite. He groaned in pleasure as the sweet, buttery taste melted on his tongue, and then he opened his eyes and looked around to see if anyone had caught the nearly-orgasmic sound he'd made. *Shit.* He'd been celibate for far too long if he enjoyed a chocolaty treat so much. He was thankful to find himself alone. The only time he liked being noisy was when he was howling at the moon or pleasuring a woman, and since he'd gotten tired of one-night-stands and getting naked with women who weren't his truemate, he hadn't taken that kind of pleasure in awhile. A long while. He was a damn monk for all intents and purposes.

There were she-wolves in his old pack who had wanted to be with him just because he was the biggest and the baddest. They liked his tattoos and his Harley and his bad attitude. Younger and stupid, he'd not minded bar brawls—hell, he'd started plenty of them over petty slights—and he never walked away from a fight. When he joined the Tressel Pack last fall, he'd hoped for a fresh start. He'd ditched his bike and bought a pickup, got a respectable job as a bouncer at the pack-run bar, and he'd done his damnedest to show others that there was something underneath the tattoos and the muscles, a male of worth. The single she-wolves in the pack, and the human women who frequented the bar, took one look at him and went ape-shit. He'd known right then that not only was his truemate *not* to be found in the Tressel Pack, but also the slightly more depressing truth that he might never find the one woman meant for him. But he'd rather be lonely than stuck in a mating with a she-wolf who wasn't his truemate, which brought him back to his current celibacy. A few years ago, if someone had told him he'd choose to be alone at night rather than find a warm body to enjoy, he'd have laughed his ass off. Now … not so much.

His thoughts were interrupted when he heard Karly say, "Excuse me, we're closed."

Logan dropped the croissant and charged into the dining room as Reika gasped in alarm. Logan snatched both women by their shirts and shoved them behind himself. "Get in the fucking office and lock the door! Call the garage!" he bellowed, pushing his arms back and shoving blindly at the women as three tall, lanky men strode through the restaurant as if they belonged there. He took in a quick breath and smelled that they were lynxes.

He glanced at the young wolves around the restaurant, counting five. Only two were older than eighteen, and they eased away from where they were and joined Logan. The other three held still, and he was grateful. They were too young to have much experience fighting and would only get hurt.

Cracking his knuckles, he said, "Leave on your own now, or I'll make you leave."

"Just you and some pups, dog? Do you really think you can take us?" the one in the middle said with a sneer.

"Yes. Get the fuck out of here now. Last warning."

The one on the right pulled a blade from his back pocket and flipped it open, waving it lightly. "Send out the she-wolf, and no one gets hurt."

"Go to hell." Logan growled, settling onto his back leg and letting his beast free enough to give him more strength and speed. His wolf was aching for a good fight, and three arrogant cats who thought a she-wolf was property and not a person were perfect.

As the one with the blade tensed to throw it, Logan jerked a chair off the floor and threw it at the lynxes, following quickly with two more chairs. They dodged out of the way, and Logan charged, crashing into the nearest cat. His momentum shoved the cat through one of the glass front doors, which shattered on impact, and Logan stopped just short of falling on his face on top of the cat as he landed on the sidewalk.

He heard the sound of clothes tearing and wolves growling and knew the two oldest boys had shifted to help. He looked at the three younger boys inside and shouted, "Guard the office door!"

Hauling the cat up by his ponytail, Logan fisted his pants with his other hand and tossed him down the sidewalk where he landed hard and rolled several times before coming to a stop against a parking meter. With a growl in his throat, he turned to go back into the restaurant as the two cats tore out of the broken front door, looked around wildly for their friend, and raced to the fallen lynx.

Logan watched them help him up and move to a truck idling down the street, taking off with a squeal of tires as police sirens filled the air. Logan walked back into the restaurant, stepping through the broken door, and moved straight to the two young wolves who had shifted. Relief slipped through him when he saw they weren't badly injured. They'd be bruised most likely; those lynxes had really been smacking them around, but it was hard to fight against a snarling wolf when they were in their human form. For whatever reason, the lynxes hadn't shifted, which was good for the young wolves.

He ruffled the heads of the two wolves and smiled. "You guys did great. Jason will be so proud of you. *I'm* proud of you both."

The wolves bristled with pride, and Logan chucked them under their chins and straightened as the police came in, guns drawn.

"They're gone, Chief," Logan told Trick. "Beat up red pickup, missing license plate. Girls are in the office."

"Good thing you were here, Logan," Trick said as he holstered his weapon.

The office door opened when one of the young wolves knocked and told the girls that it was safe to come out. Just as Karly and Reika stepped out of the office, Linus and Bo rushed into the restaurant.

Linus grabbed Karly in a tight hug, and she started to cry. Logan watched as Bo came close to Reika, touched her shoulder and asked if she was okay, but did nothing more. Logan was certain that Bo wanted to hold Reika, to reassure himself that she was safe now, but he held back.

Bo turned to look at him. "Thank you, Logan."

Linus looked over Karly's head, his face twisted in worry, relief, and anger. "Thank you."

Logan nodded. "It was a good thing you asked me to be here. They weren't counting on anyone being here except the girls and the young males. I don't know how they knew. Maybe they were watching around town."

Bo frowned. Reika gripped Bo's arm, and he looked down at her. She looked like she was about to lose it, but she managed to say, with a voice that only slightly quivered, "Please don't make me stay with anyone else anymore, Bo. I couldn't stand it if someone got hurt because of me."

"I won't, Reika," Bo promised.

Reika looked at Logan. "Thank you. I was frozen. If you hadn't been here, I don't know what would have happened."

"I'm glad I was here. I'm going to talk to Trick. I'll check in with you later."

Bo nodded, spoke to Reika and then Linus and Karly, and then he was gone, with Reika. After Logan gave his statement to Trick, he talked to Jason and Michael, who had come from the garage when Karly called. Logan explained what happened, praised the young wolves for their help, and volunteered to help patrol around town during the day. He and Teller had been driving around at night, using the garage's tow trucks, but obviously the lynxes were either getting desperate or becoming more arrogant.

Later that day, as he patrolled around town with a young wolf named Dante, he checked in with Bo, who said that Reika was shaken but unharmed, and that was the most important thing.

"Did I say thank you, Logan? It's kind of a blur," Bo said.

"Yeah, you did, and you're welcome. If she were my woman, I'd trust you to return the favor."

Bo hesitated, "Logan, she's not—"

Logan snorted and cut him off. "Okay, Bo. Keep telling yourself that."

Bo was silent for several moments, and then he sighed loudly. "It's one giant cluster-fuck."

"Life is like that sometimes. Don't forget that there are a lot of wolves who would love to find their truemates." *Like me.*

"I know."

Logan could hear the hurt in Bo's voice. Logan wasn't much of a soft, romantic guy, but he knew that Bo was already head-over-heels for Reika, and his plan to set her free from the lynxes and then send her on her merry way was going to kill him.

"Love's hard as fuck, yeah?" Logan said, finally.

"Yeah."

Still it was a hardship he wished he could suffer through. Leaving the restaurant, he parked the tow truck at the garage and headed home to catch a nap before his shift at the bar. Somewhere out in the world was his own truemate, and he hoped to hell he'd meet her soon.

Chapter Seven

Bo didn't think that anything had ever struck him dead with terror the way that the news that the lynxes were at the restaurant had. Linus had answered his cell and grabbed Bo's shoulder before Karly even finished explaining the situation, and the two of them had driven as fast as they could to the renovated restaurant. They'd passed the lynxes' truck as it shot down the street away from the scene, and they only let the lynxes go without chase because they knew that Karly and Reika were safely locked inside the office and hadn't been taken.

Bo had never been more grateful for Logan's friendship and the young wolves, as well, who had held their own even though they'd been scared. Jason was planning to honor the young wolves at the February full moon celebration for their bravery.

As soon as Trick had interviewed Reika and said she could leave, Linus gave Bo his keys, and Bo drove Linus' truck back to the garage. Bo left the keys at the front desk with Cades and took Reika home. Reika sat tense in the seat next to him, chewing her bottom lip and gripping the door handle tight enough to make her knuckles white.

He opened the front door and let Reika into the house and then hung up both of their coats. Just as he turned to ask her to sit down so they could talk, there was a knock at the door.

A glance through the peep-hole showed Teller standing on the porch with a dark duffel bag. When he opened the door, Teller stepped inside.

Reika gasped, "Oh, my bag!"

Teller handed it to her, and she hugged the bag to her chest and smiled at both of them, tears glistening in her eyes. "Thank you so much!"

"It was my pleasure. Your car was about two hours northwest of Allen, in a community park in a small town called Belvin. The lynxes were obviously here in town when I went to pick it up because although I could smell them all over it, I never saw them. They did rifle through the bag and dump the contents on the floor, but I checked everything carefully for GPS trackers and found none on the contents or on the bag itself."

Reika made a face. "I don't like to think of them touching my stuff."

Bo smiled at her and reached out, stroking his fingers down her arm. "You can wash your clothes and the bag."

She nodded, smiled once more at Teller, and then took the bag into the bedroom.

Teller watched her walk away and then turned to Bo. "Jason contacted the Were-Animal Alliance and told them that Reika was here with us and under our protection. The two wolves who were attacked survived and are recovering with their home pack that is part of the WAA. They were planning to bring her back to their home pack and give her a new identity and everything."

Bo nodded. "She'll be glad to know they're alive."

"I'm sure. That had to weigh heavily on her mind. But from what the guy who runs the WAA said, the packs that go in to retrieve wolves in trouble know that they could get hurt or even killed doing it, and they do it because they choose to."

Bo reached for his wallet. "How much do I owe you for returning her car?"

Teller shook his head. "Don't worry about it. I took care of it for you."

"Thanks. I'll let Reika know, too."

Teller put his hand on the door knob and said, "Logan and I are going to be taking patrol shifts, and we've got Trick and his deputies watching the streets for any signs of the lynxes. A few of the retired wolves are also driving around for a few hours at a time. We'll do our best to keep an eye out for the lynxes."

"I'm keeping her home from now on, at least until I can get things squared away. A handful of wolves are going to stand guard here tomorrow so I can finish the one project, and then I'll be here to keep an eye on her."

"Let me know if you need anything."

Bo clapped him on the back. "Thanks, T."

Locking the door behind his friend, Bo walked back into the bedroom and found Reika sitting on the bed with a worn book in her hand.

She looked up at him and said, "I'm glad the two wolves are okay."

"Me, too. What book is that?" He joined her on the bed.

"My favorite. *The Princess Bride*. Ever read it?"

He took it from her hands and turned it over, noticing the dog-eared pages and the cracked spine. "Only if it came in comic book form. I wasn't much for reading growing up. I was all about the pack and learning how to fight. How about you?" He gave her back the book, and she hugged it to her chest. "What were you like in high school?"

She settled the full weight of her beautiful blue eyes on him, and for a moment he didn't think his heart was beating at all. "I was pretty lonely. No one really wanted to get close to me because of the lynxes. The pack was there for me, of course, but I always felt like a shadow was dogging me my whole life. My family were the only ones who never looked at me like I was damaged goods."

He snorted inwardly. She wasn't damaged. *He* was the very definition of the word. "You're strong and compassionate, Reika, not damaged. You got dealt a shit hand, and I'm going to find a way out of the mess you're in so you can have your life back."

She opened her mouth to protest, and he silenced her with a swift kiss. Standing up before she could tell him not to fight for her, he told her he was going to make something for lunch, and he'd call her when it was ready.

They spent the day together, talking some but mostly just watching TV. Later, when they sat next to each other on the couch, she asked him about his leg, and he told her the story. She listened in silence, tearing up over his old wounds and making his heart squeeze painfully in his chest. When he was finished, she hugged him tightly but said nothing else.

When night fell, she came right out of the bedroom in her pajamas and curled up against him. He was growing accustomed to the sweet scent of her and the slight weight as she lay against him. It was going to be hell to watch her leave.

Friday morning, he left Reika in the house after securing a promise from her that she would not try to leave and headed to work. Five wolves were standing guard at the house, including Peter Gerrick and his wife, Tina, who stayed inside the house with Reika to keep her company. Bo got straight to work so he could leave as soon as possible, but his stomach growled loudly around eleven, and Michael suggested they go for a walk to the deli and get something to eat. Then Michael offered to help Bo finish up so he could head home.

At Pete's Garage, Bo worked on restorations. His father had been a classic car buff, and Bo had spent his summers helping him fix up cars, restoring them to their former glory. At the moment, he was restoring the air conditioner on a '77 Corvette. The owner was anxious to have it ready to go for summer, and it was one of the last things that needed to be done before it was finished.

When he walked down the street with Michael to grab a sandwich from the deli, he saw Jazlyn, a she-wolf who worked at Jake's and sang for the house band. She was mated to Fritz, who had been part of the Tressel Pack before he left to go rogue with Jazlyn and her brothers.

Jazlyn walked down the street quickly, a paper grocery sack in one arm. Three tall, lanky males stepped from an alley, and Bo's wolf howled in dismay. The lynxes! One of them snagged Jazlyn by the neck, and the other two stalked towards Michael and Bo.

Bo and Michael let their beasts rise. Jazlyn shrieked and tried to wiggle free of the male holding her, but he held her slight form as easily as a doll.

"Let her go, asshole. Your beef is with me," Bo growled.

"Bring us our woman, and we'll be happy to leave," one of the two closer ones said.

The third one licked his lips as he looked over his shoulder at Jazlyn, who was struggling valiantly. "We'll just take her with us. An insurance policy to make sure you bring our property to us."

"The hell you will." Bo snarled at the way they called Reika their property and settled into his wolf, feeling Michael do the same. They both launched themselves towards the males at the same time, tackling the two swiftly and rolling them to the ground. They were fast, though, and darted up to their feet, dancing on the balls of their feet as if they hadn't been knocked hard to the pavement.

There was a strange grunting sound, and Bo's head snapped to the side as Jazlyn's brother Shayne squeezed the neck of the male holding Jazlyn until he released her. Shayne was nearly seven feet tall, incredibly muscular, and broad. Jazlyn fell to the ground, and Michael raced forward, helping her to her feet. Shayne raised the male off the ground by a foot and slammed him against the wall of a building. The male's eyes rolled back in his head as his face turned from bright red to purple from lack of oxygen. Shayne growled, slammed him to the wall once more, and then dropped him like a heap of dirty laundry.

He turned towards the two males who stood staring in shock. Raising a hand, Shayne growled, "Leave."

The males snapped to attention, grabbed their brother, and carried him to a waiting vehicle in the park across the street from the garage. To Bo's dismay, he saw that it was a dark blue sedan and not the rundown pickup they'd been driving. No wonder they'd been able to get into town unnoticed; they'd switched vehicles. The car was also missing plates, which made Bo wonder if it was stolen.

"Are you okay, Jazlyn?" Bo asked, helping to collect the items from her bag.

She rubbed at her neck. "Yeah. Thank you for sticking up for me. Who are those guys? They smell weird."

Shayne took the bag from Bo and put his large hand on her shoulder. "Lynxes," he said darkly.

Bo nodded and gave them a quick run-down of the situation. "I'm sorry that you got caught in the middle," Bo said to Jazlyn.

"It's not your fault. They're bastards for what they're trying to do to your mate. If you need our pack's help, you just call."

Shayne nodded solemnly and turned his sister away from them and resumed their walk.

Bo called his house immediately and talked to Peter, making sure he was on alert. Then he called Teller and told him about the new vehicle, which made his friend shout obscenities loud enough that he had to pull the phone from his ear.

Shaking out the worry that settled in his gut, Bo and Michael walked to the deli. "She's your truemate," Michael said, as they leaned against the counter and waited for their sandwiches.

"It doesn't matter," Bo said, cracking the lid on a soda.

"The fuck it doesn't. You know you're the only one who can break the promise."

"Of course I'm going to do that," Bo said irritably. "I mean, it doesn't matter after she's free. She needs a male of worth."

Michael put a hand on Bo's shoulder. "You *are* a male of worth."

"I'm going to lose my ability to shift in a few years. What kind of mate would I be? I wouldn't even be able to help her if she was in trouble on a hunt. I'd be sitting home with the non-shifters, cut down before my prime. What kind of life would that be for her?"

"I think you should let *her* make that decision."

Bo shrugged, grabbing for his wrapped sandwich. He was afraid to think about offering her the chance to be his truemate. Because if he never told her the truth about his feelings for her, then he never had to face her rejection. And that rejection would be more than he could bear.

He finished his sandwich, and with Michael's help, he completed the restoration within two hours and headed home. He had some vacation time saved up, and he'd already cleared it with Jason to take time off. He wasn't sure what he needed to do to break the blood-debt, and Reika wasn't inclined to tell him what it was. He knew that she was trying to protect him.

Reika was twitchy enough about innocents being harmed in abstract, so he chose not to tell her about running into the lynxes on the street. He didn't want to tell her that her fears were coming true.

He brought home groceries and helped Reika make dinner. He asked her about her life, but she had grown quieter as dinner progressed and began answering his questions with no more than one or two words. He could practically feel her pulling away from him, and it made him ache.

That night she slept with him on the couch again, which confused him. And aroused the hell out of him. Why she insisted on cuddling up to him, even though he coveted it, didn't make sense to him. He was certain she was looking for a way get away from him and strike out on her own, but he couldn't let that happen.

The next few days passed much the same. The lynxes didn't show up again, but Bo knew they were most likely just licking their wounds for a re-group. It grew more and more difficult to keep his wolf at bay around her. Every morning he woke to her in his arms, her sweet scent surrounding him. And then darkness came, and she would stretch out with him, her smaller form against him, her lush body pressed close. He'd slept well since she'd been there, but he wasn't sure exactly what it was about her that calmed his aches.

Monday night, his phone roused him from sleep. He dug it out of his pocket and answered with a grumble.

"Are you and Reika safe?" Jason asked.

He sat up, his wolf on sudden alert. "Yes. What happened?"

"Teller was patrolling through town, and he saw the three males slinking around the garage."

Bo's stomach filled with lead. That garage had been in Jason's family for generations. "Did they do anything?"

"Teller alerted Trick and me before he found out what they were doing. They had set a small fire in the back, jimmying the back door open and tossing accelerant inside. Trick and Teller put the fire out before too much damage was done, but I thought you should know something else."

"Tell me no one was hurt."

"No, the garage was completely empty. But they tacked a note to the door that says, *'Give us back our woman or the whole town burns.'*"

The silence was deafening. Bo and Jason had spoken many times in the last few days about what the next steps should be, if the lynxes retaliated again.

"I'm ready, Jason," Bo said with conviction.

"I'll make the calls. How much time do you need?"

He glanced down at Reika, whose beautiful features were carved with worry. "Five days."

"See you then."

Bo hung up and leaned on his elbow, looking down at her. He knew with her superior hearing that she had heard every word. "Was anyone hurt?"

"No, sweetheart. Teller called the police chief who is mated to one of our female wolves, and the two of them put the fire out before there was too much damage. No one was there, and the damage was minimal."

She took in a shaky breath. "I need to leave."

He bristled, man and wolf. "Hell no. It's even more dangerous now."

"Bo, please," she started, and he silenced her with his mouth. He and his pack would see to it that she was safe for the next five days. Plans had been made and set in place. All he had to do was keep her from trying to run on her own, and everything would be fine.

He hoped.

Chapter Eight

Bo's warm mouth was insistent against hers as he leaned into her, sweeping his tongue along the seam. Her mouth parted, and their tongues met in a sensual slide that made her skin tingle. She'd been fighting her attraction to Bo, and not very successfully. She knew he wanted to try to break the promise between her and the lynx males, but she couldn't risk that happening. Not now. Not when he'd come to mean so much to her.

He moved off the couch, not breaking their embrace, and lifted her up in his arms. He carried her through the house to the bedroom, and she felt the strain of his injured leg as he walked. An idea formed in her mind as he laid her down on the bed. She could heal him. She *would* heal him, and then she would leave. He would be better off healed and able to move on with his life, even though her wolf howled in anguish in her mind at the thought of leaving him.

Gorgeous.

Kind.

Sweet.

Hers.

His lips trailed down her cheek as he covered her with his body. She ran her blunt nails up his broad back, feeling the muscles as they bunched and moved under her fingers. His teeth pressed down on her ear lobe and then found the sensitive patch of skin behind her ear. He licked a path from that spot down her neck, and she arched under him, her hands grasping at him.

The thin shirt she wore to bed was pushed up and her bare breasts chilled in the cooler air. He licked across one nipple while his hands explored the lush mounds. He grabbed the nipple between his teeth and tugged gently, the teasing pressure making her body ache.

She ran her fingers through his hair, testing the soft strands. Her body grew tight and heat bloomed in her core, as he turned his attention to her neglected nipple and tugged and licked it until it was as hot and hard as the other one.

He kissed down her belly, circling his tongue around her navel, and kissing along the edge of her pajama pants. The ribbon drawstring came undone slowly, and he tugged them and her panties down her hips. She watched him toss them away, never taking his eyes off her body.

He pushed her legs apart and stretched out between them, trailing his fingers along her heated skin as he propped himself above her on one arm. Her skin prickled under his touch.

His fingers grazed the neatly trimmed hair of her pussy, and she bit her lip. "Fuck you smell good, Reika," he groaned, and it came out vibrating with a growl.

One finger parted her sex ever so slightly, circling her clit slowly. With thumb and finger, he parted her, exposing her completely. Laid bare before him, she watched his hazel eyes darken with pure lust. He lowered his head and stroked the flat of his tongue up her slit. She groaned as he lifted her leg over his shoulder, spreading her further open. He licked at her, lapped at her, wiggled his tongue inside her as she moaned and gripped the blanket. His tongue moved to her clit, the tip flicking over her sensitive bud as two fingers pushed inside her. Her hips rocked, wanting him deeper, as he began to rub and press his fingers against her heated, honeyed walls. Her stomach began to flutter. He sucked on her clit, pulling the bud deep into his mouth and then releasing it to flick and tease with his tongue.

His searching fingers struck heaven, and she gasped, "Oh there, there!" His fingers rubbed her fast, and she felt her body flood as pleasure spiraled through her. With a cry of pure bliss, she came, tension coiling in her limbs as his fingers worked her harder, faster, and his lips closed over her sensitive bud. The pleasure never ended, it just built and built, as he drove her forward into another place, where time stopped and everything in her body went liquid.

"Bo!" she shrieked when the second orgasm slammed down on her, her vision edged with sparks.

He moved off the bed, and she heard the pop of his button and the grating of his zipper being lowered, and then he jerked her towards him by her legs, positioning himself between her thighs as he stood on the floor. His hands landed on her hips as she curled her legs around his waist and he slammed into her. Her eyes rolled back in her head. Nothing had ever felt so right, so perfect.

Pounding into her, he groaned, squeezing her hips as his cock thrust home again and again. Their eyes met and held. His were flickering from hazel to amber, his lips parted as he panted for breath. Sweat glistened on their bodies, and the scent of them together lingered on the air.

She lifted her legs higher on his hips, gripping his arms and meeting his thrusts. She panted his name, pleading for more, wanting more, needing everything he could give her.

Pleasure wove through her as he increased his pace, slamming his body against hers. She cried out when her body tightened around him, and he shouted her name, pumping into her as he arched his back, tossing his head back with a howl of pure bliss.

Eyes half lidded, he moved her up the bed and collapsed next to her, rolling her body on top of his with a sultry groan.

She'd *never* experienced anything like that before. She'd had orgasms during sex before, but never so powerful. She felt like her insides had been turned to liquid, and she was tingly warm, from her head down to her toes. She settled her head on his shoulder, laying one arm across his heaving chest and stretching one leg between his. His cock lay glistening and still semi-hard, visible through the open zipper of his jeans.

Reika frowned as she once more felt the scratch of Bo's jeans against her legs. She'd never been with a guy who kept his pants on during sex. Even though it had been amazing, she could feel his injury holding him back, causing him pain while he tried to bring her pleasure.

There's only one thing to do. It's the least I can do, since I'm leaving.

She rolled to her knees and hooked her fingers into the waistband of his jeans and tugged. His hands shot out, and the sleepy, sexy look disappeared from his face. "Don't."

She tugged again, but his grip on her wrists tightened. "Bo, I can help you. Let me see your leg."

"I haven't let anyone except a doctor see my leg in the last five years. I'm not going to start now, Reika." His voice lowered, and his face shadowed darkly. She had the power to heal him, and she was going to do it whether he liked it or not.

She called her beast, and her claws sprang from her fingertips. The sudden surge in power from her beast made her stronger than him in his human form, and she pulled from his grasp and dragged her claws down the fabric of his jeans, shredding them without touching his skin.

"Fuck, Reika!" Bo shouted, scrambling from the bed. He held the scraps of his jeans up around his legs, desperately trying to keep the material covering his right leg.

She let out an unhappy growl and retracted her claws. "I can feel how much pain you're in. I'm an apex. Let me heal you."

His hands tightened on the material, and he dropped his head. "I don't want you to see me, Reika."

She climbed off the bed, determined to help him. He'd done so much for her this past week, and she could do this one thing for him. He stepped away from her, still holding onto the jeans. They moved around the bedroom, him taking a step backwards as she tried to move closer to him, until she wanted to scream.

She'd had enough. Drawing on her wolf once more, she growled to Bo, "Whatever you do, fight your shift until I tell you otherwise."

"What?" He stopped moving and stared at her in confusion, as she slipped down to the floor and shifted. Her lightly tanned skin split as silky black fur grew thickly. Her bones snapped and reformed, faster than the human eye could process, and she snapped her jaws twice and shook her whole body out. She sat on her haunches for only long enough to secrete the healing venom on her tongue. She licked each claw on both front paws, the venom glistening on her thick claws, the very essence of what made her a healer.

Bo stood still like a statue, his head cocked to the side as he stared at her. She hoped he remembered her command not to shift. If he shifted before her venom had a chance to work, the healing would be incomplete. It would be painful either way, but going through the pain of healing and not being whole on the other side of it was inconceivable.

With a short growl, she sprang at him, her front claws slashing down the length of his right leg. He roared in alarm and pain, tumbling backwards as her body landed on him and knocked the breath out of his lungs. Digging her front claws into the meat of his legs, where she could feel the worst of his injury, he howled under her, shoving at her as she flexed her venom-soaked claws deeper into the old wounds.

She snapped her jaws down on his shoulder, deep into the muscles. Her healing venom flowed freely into his body now, carried into the blood stream, fast on the path to healing him. She kept her jaws locked on him, not only to keep more healing venom flowing into him, but also to keep him from shifting. His body shook and jerked under her and he struggled, but he was no match for her as she straddled his body.

Her senses picked up the changes in his body as the venom in her claws worked through the muscles, healing and repairing damage that had caused him pain for so long. She knew his story and knew that she'd been brought into his life for this reason. No one should suffer his entire life for one bad mistake in his youth.

His body locked up as the venom healed. She released him once she was certain he had plenty of venom in his body. She nuzzled the fabric of his jeans out of the way and looked at what remained of the scars of his youth. She had split his leg open from hip to ankle with two well placed slashes of her paws, digging her claws into the worst of the injury.

His mouth worked silently, and a single tear escaped his tightly closed eyes. She knew from what others had told her that there was no pain quite like an apex healing. She only hoped he forgave her when he could walk and shift without his old pains.

Stretching out next to him, she licked the tear from his cheek and nuzzled his neck, amazed at his resilience as he continued to stay in his human form and not give in to the shift. For wolves, when pain in their human form became too great, the wolf tended to want to spring free. Holding onto the wolf while pain rode his body would be one of the most difficult things that Bo would ever do. Pride wove through her as she watched his muscles tense harder and harder until he was like a string stretched taut.

An hour passed. Two.

She watched him intently as he wrestled with the pain as her venom forced his body to heal at an accelerated rate. As she marveled at his strength and determination, she thought over her growing feelings for him. Ever since they had made love, she'd fought her own battle over leaving him behind. Her wolf wanted to mate with him and stay in Allen forever, but the rational part of her mind knew that was selfish. If she stayed, she was sending Bo to his death at the hands of those sadistic males. It would be the most difficult thing she had ever done, but she would walk away from him. To save him. To set him free. She would rather suffer alone for the rest of her life than know that her selfish heart had gotten him killed.

There would be no other male for her for the span of her life but him, and she would do anything to see him safe. Even if that meant running away.

With her heart breaking, Reika shifted into her human form and knelt next to Bo. "Shift, baby, please. It's been long enough."

Bo's eyes were bright amber when he cracked them open, his lips drawn tightly, and he let out a hard breath and shifted. Within minutes, a dark gray wolf rolled onto four paws and howled, and then stalked right for her.

Chapter Nine

Bo had thought the most painful thing he'd ever had happen was the accident and the follow-up surgeries. Reika's healing abilities were far, far worse. It was as if she had injected his body with acid and then told him to just hang out while it obliterated him. His first instinct had been to shift, when her claws were digging into his leg and the first pains had begun like little flames licking at his muscles. He'd remembered her words and had been determined not to shift. He knew he could trust her. He loved her, after all, and he couldn't really love someone he didn't trust.

When her jaws clamped down on his shoulder, he'd been caught between pleasure and pain. She'd marked him, whether she meant it that way or not, and he just hoped like hell that the marks lingered. When wolves marked in their wolf forms, it was serious business. She'd just made it known that he was hers.

As she stayed right by his side while he fought against the urge to shift, an idea formed in his mind. If she was really healing him, if his body would really be whole, then he would use it to keep her here. There was nothing wrong with a little seduction, a few dozen orgasms, maybe, to make her admit that she loved him, that she was his mate, and that she was going to stay. No matter the threat that stretched over them from the lynx clan, he knew in his heart that he could protect her. His wolf would not allow her to be taken. And once she was free of the blood-debt, he would claim her as his truemate forever.

After the lynxes had attacked Jazlyn, Bo knew it was just a matter of time before they recovered and attacked again. He and Jason had spoken at length about the situation and decided the best thing to do was to go challenge the lynx males for Reika. Bo was her truemate; they belonged together. It wasn't even a matter of him letting her go anymore; she was ingrained too deeply into his heart and soul. Hell, she *was* his heart and soul. When Jason had called about the garage, Bo told him he was ready for the plan to be implemented. As alpha, Jason would have called Reika's alpha and asked him to speak to the lynx leader. If the lynxes would back off for five days, Bo would bring Reika to her home pack and challenge them for her. They would use the time to travel, but mostly, Bo was going to get the idea of her running off on her own out of her mind. If he had to drown her in pleasure to get her to admit to being his, then he'd just jump on that grenade.

He stalked towards her in his wolf form as she sat, naked, on his bedroom floor. Her eyes were shiny with unshed tears, and she sniffled and leaned forward, running her fingers through his thick coat. "Feel better, baby?"

He nuzzled her neck and licked at her pulse. She shivered and wrapped her arms around his neck. He let out a long sigh and then took in a deep breath, letting the sweet scent of her wash over him. He loved how she smelled, how she tasted. He didn't think there was anything that tasted better in this world than his woman when she came on his tongue.

He sat back on his haunches and regarded her. Their eyes met, her dark blue and his wolf-amber. She looked happy, but he could see the turmoil in her eyes. She was torn. She'd probably decided to heal him so he'd have something nice to remember her by. Well, she had his heart now, and he wasn't just going to let her walk away with it.

They moved to the kitchen, and she tossed him one of the steaks he'd planned to grill for her for dinner. He caught the meat in his jaws and settled down to eat, amazed at the ease with which his right leg moved now. No tightened muscles screaming for relief, no desire to gnaw his own leg off. When the steak was gone, he nosed his leg. He was pleased to find her scent lingered on him.

"It's the healing venom, Bo." She sat down on the floor while he ate, with her arms wrapped around her knees. "When I'm in my form, I can secrete a healing essence. If a wound is small enough, I can lick it and it will heal. For bigger wounds, I can bite, and the venom goes into the blood stream and helps heal. But in your case, I wanted to put the venom directly into your wound and bite you as well, since it's so old."

He hummed in his throat, which came out sounding like a wolfy purr. He could practically taste her nervousness. He imagined she was worried he would be pissed off at the pain the healing had caused. The phrase "no pain, no gain" floated through his mind. He certainly didn't fault her for what she had done, and now that he could feel his body getting back on track, he fell a little bit more in love with her than he had when he'd been buried to the hilt in her hot body.

He licked her neck again, growling softly, and turned around and headed towards the back door. Standing at the back door, he felt a little bit like an idiot, but he barked and scratched until she stood next to him, grinning.

"What's that, boy? Did Timmy fall down the well?" She was grinning so hard her cheeks had to hurt.

He huffed and nipped at her bare knee, and she laughed, pushing open the sliding back door. "I'm going to grab a blanket and sit out on the porch. Have a good run, baby."

He barked once and leapt off the porch. He wasn't going to go far, or even leave his yard. There was always a chance the lynx males might come here, although he doubted it. They'd not tracked him to the house yet, and at this point, their leader would have called them home. They were determined to have his woman, and there was no way in hell he would allow that as long as he had a breath left in his body.

He felt like a puppy. Or, rather, since werewolves didn't shift until they were adults, he imagined he felt like a real wolf puppy might feel—as if the world was new and his for the taking. He leapt and hopped, stretching his right leg and not feeling the familiar painful twinge that always made his breath catch in his throat. He roused a rabbit from a hole near the back of his property and chased it as it darted around the yard, not really interested in catching it.

He turned as the door shut, and his sexy sweetheart, wrapped in a thick blanket, sat down in the old rocker that had belonged to his grandfather. Fuck, he loved her. He felt his heart swell, and it filled his chest, rumbling out of his throat with a long, low growl. Now he understood what his friends meant when they said that love changed everything. He'd never considered himself selfish, but now he wanted to give her everything, including freeing her from the promise to the lynx males.

He stretched out on the snow and rolled around a few times, digging his claws into the hard ground and launching himself around the yard. If he could grin in his shift, he would be grinning like a mad fool right now, but he didn't care. His woman had given him back his life and his heart. He couldn't love her more than he did at that moment.

She fidgeted on the rocker, and even on the cold air, the scent of her arousal pulsed at him, and his wolf growled in happiness. *Mark her. Make her ours forever!*

He stalked towards her, breathing in the deep, hot scent of her. Shifting easily, for the first time in his life, his body changed rapidly from wolf to human, and he climbed the steps, grabbing a hunk of snow in one hand, before falling to his knees in front of her. Dropping the tightly packed snow to the porch, he drew her legs out from the blanket and lifted her knees, spreading them apart and hooking them over the arms of the rocker. She gasped and moaned as the brisk air touched her heated flesh, pink and wet and throbbing, just for him.

"You look like you've got wicked things on your mind, baby," she crooned, running her fingers through his hair.

"I'm getting revenge on you for that Lassie crack earlier." He leaned forward and licked her pussy in one slow stroke, from the bottom of her hot, dripping slit, to the tight, needy pearl of her clit. "Oh yeah, and I'm thanking you for healing me."

Her body lifted for him, and she dug her fingers into his scalp. "You are very welcome." Biting her lip and closing her eyes, he watched her head fall back and bliss light her features as he stroked his tongue across her heated folds again. She tasted incredible. As sultry as a summer night and as sweet as the first flower to bloom in spring. He tilted his head and swiped his tongue around the edges of her entrance, probing the depths with his tongue lightly, caressing and teasing. He ignored the incessant tug on his hair from her fingers, relishing the pleasure soaked whimpers that seeped from her throat.

He reached for the snow he had captured in his hand. The pressure of it being held in his palm had created a small icy phallus, just the thing that she needed to help her cool down a little. With the fingers of one hand he pulled the flesh around her clit taut, exposing the bundle of nerves. He deviled it with his tongue, casting his eyes up the length of her body and finding her digging her teeth into her bottom lip as she panted and groaned softly. He laved her clit once and then ran the end of the packed snow across her tender bud, and she jerked, her blue eyes popping open.

He sucked her cold clit until it was hot and wet, and then applied the ice to it. He alternated the heat and cold until her legs trembled and a tiny bead of blood dotted her lip where she'd dug her teeth into it. Tossing the nearly melted ice aside, he thrust his cold fingers into her body and clamped his lips around her clit, sucking hard on the needy bud until she shrieked in pleasure, her body wild beneath him. He jerked upright, pushing the rocker backwards until it met the wall of the house, and he thrust his cock into her waiting pussy, feeling the sweet wetness of her body as she pulsed around him in the throes of her orgasm.

He kept himself above her with his hands on the spindles of the rocker and fucked her hard as her hands pulled his mouth down to hers, and she sucked his tongue into her mouth. He tasted the bit of blood on her tongue from where she had swiped it across her lip, and his wolf went nuts as his body slammed into hers with speed and force. Until there was nothing but the two of them. Their bodies meeting, their tongues tangled, and the splintering sound of the rocker as he found release in her pussy and she followed, milking him hard.

Easing back, he righted the rocker and winced at the creaking sound, noticing the splinters on the porch. Well, he hadn't exactly expected an eighty-year-old rocker to be able to handle a sound fucking from an impassioned wolf, had he?

He picked Reika up in his arms, loving the glazed look in her eyes and the flush on her skin. He carried her straight into his bathroom and flipped the water on, closing the drain so the old-fashioned clawfoot tub would fill. Keeping her tight against him with one arm, he adjusted the water until it was just a shade under too-hot and stepped into the tub.

Her body nestled nicely right in front of him, his legs on either side of hers and her back to his chest. They watched the water fill the tub in silence as he stroked her arms lightly, and she rested her head on his bicep.

The water reached their hips, and she sighed deeply, "That's better."

Chuckling, he scooped water up in one hand and let it dribble down her slit. "A little cold, sweetheart?"

She hummed in her throat. "There was this crazy wolf who tried to freeze my clit off."

"Just crazy about you." He nuzzled her cheek and kissed her ear. Tipping her chin until she looked at him he said, "I am, you know. Crazy about you."

"Bo, I—" she started, and he sensed she was about to pull away.

Stopping her before she could say anything that might damage his self-esteem, he brushed her lips with his finger. "You don't have to say it back, sweetheart. Just hear me say it. I love you. I know you're mine, my truemate. And I'll do anything to keep you safe and keep you forever."

Her eyes widened and the glitter of tears shone before she closed them and settled her head back on his bicep. If he couldn't feel that she was meant to be his mate, he might have felt her rejection as a crushing blow. But he knew she wanted to get away from the threat of the lynxes and that she wanted to keep him safe as well. In her mind, leaving was the only way to do both of those things, and she didn't want him to lose all that he had. The only way he'd lose everything was if he lost her.

They soaked in the tub in silence, washing each other eventually with soap and making love on the bed. This time he was not only completely naked with her, but he lay with her on the bed, not forced to stand because his leg ached. His leg now had two sets of claw marks on it, but they were fading to a color just slightly lighter than his natural tan. The long twisted scars of his injury and surgeries were gone, and he would wear these marks with pride because they came from his woman.

He'd been happy to see that the marks on his shoulder from her teeth were still there, a curve of dots from where each tooth broke through the skin on either side of his shoulder. She had passed out quickly after they made love, and he waited until she was sound asleep before he put his plan into action.

He dressed quickly and packed a bag for them, running out to the truck and turning it on so the heater would have time to warm up the cab before he put his sweetheart inside.

With two boxes of groceries and a battery charger for his cell, he went back into the bedroom and gathered Reika in the blankets and strode out into the cold night air. Settling her still sleeping body in the passenger seat, he closed the door silently and went around to the driver's side where he climbed in and closed the door. The last thing he did before he put the truck into gear was handcuff her right wrist to the door handle. No matter what, she wasn't leaving his side until she promised that she wasn't going anywhere.

Bo had spent a lifetime seeing things he could never have because of his injured leg. He wasn't about to let his mate run off on her own on some kind of misguided mission to lure the lynxes away from town, away from him, and try to disappear on her own. He was proud as hell of her for being so noble, but he wasn't about to wimp out and let her take the fall for him.

Everything that mattered in the world to him was sitting in the seat next to him, and he'd be damned if he let three entitled, asshole lynxes get in the way of their future. Come hell or high water, Reika was his. Period.

Chapter Ten

Reika yawned and stretched, and her eyes popped open as a chain rattled and her right arm wouldn't lift over her head. She was in a truck. Bo's truck. With Bo. Handcuffed?

"Morning sunshine," he winked, looking far too sexy in a scruffy, unshaven sort of way.

"What the hell, Bo?" She jerked on the handcuff and glared at him. All her fuzzy feelings over the healing and the fantastic, bone-melting sex they'd had afterwards disappeared in a rush.

"Don't worry, honey. We're nearly there, and then I'll let you go."

"Nearly where?" Panic rose inside her like a tidal wave. Was he taking her back to the lynxes? He'd gotten his healing and a few good tumbles and he was done with her? *No!* Her wolf growled in her mind, and she knew that was the furthest thing from the truth. Bo loved her. Not only had he told her that amazing truth last night in the tub, but she could feel it. His wolf wanted to commune with hers, and her wolf was clamoring in her skull to do the same. He was her truemate, the only one who would be strong enough to break the promise that her alpha made all those years ago.

She suddenly knew where they were going.

"This won't work," she said as she tried to fold her arms and then groused at the cuff once more.

"What won't work?"

"Hiding out. They've been waiting for me since I was seven. They won't give up just because you took me somewhere, and we disappeared for a while. And besides, you have a job, don't you? Just take me back, and we'll work something out."

She tried her best to sound reassuring, but she had a feeling he knew the moment he looked away she was going to hit the road. She had to keep him safe. He was too important to her now to let him fight for her. He could die. She couldn't risk it.

"Right." He cast a side-glance at her. "So you can fuck me into a coma and slip out the back door? I don't think so, sweetheart. I know your plan, and I'm not going to let you do it."

He pulled behind a large farmhouse and drove down a barely visible dirt lane to a large, red barn. The doors were open, and the interior was filled with tractors covered in a layer of dirt and dust. "Excuse me, you're the one who fucked me into a coma. I can't believe I slept through you putting me in the truck and handcuffing me to the door!"

He winked and put the truck into park, turning off the engine. "Stay put, baby, and I'll be right back."

He got out, and she turned and watched him close the big doors. Then he moved to the back of the barn and lifted a hatch that appeared to have been hidden under a rug. After a few moments, as the air in the truck chilled and she started shivering, he returned to the truck and opened her door carefully, unlocking her cuff. Pulling her into his arms, he carried her quickly to the back of the barn and walked down a flight of wooden steps into a concrete room that was about twenty by twenty feet. One door led to what she assumed was a bathroom—or rather, what she hoped was a bathroom—and the rest of the room was furnished as a combo bedroom/kitchen/living area. It reminded her of an efficiency apartment.

He plopped her down on a large bed, and without a word, he swiftly handcuffed her to the iron headboard. "Oh really, Bo, that's hardly necessary," she huffed in indignation. "And you said you'd let me go!"

"I will, eventually. I just meant I'd let you go from the truck, not let you go forever. I'll be right back. Stay put."

"Oh, ha ha," she fumed.

He disappeared up the stairs and left her to grumble at her situation. *How the hell had he known her plans?*

He returned with a box and a duffel over his shoulder, and he deposited them on the small table in the kitchen area and walked back up the stairs. Pride flickered through her as she saw how easily he moved now. Her healing had worked.

After another box was set on the table, he pulled a handle on the door and shut it, clicking a combination lock closed, and twirling the dial. *Oh for hell's sake.*

"Fine, I get it. I'm locked in down here. So let me go." She rattled the cuff at him as he began unpacking the boxes.

Glancing over his shoulder at her, he said quietly, "Are you ready to admit that I'm your truemate? Will you swear that we're in this together and promise you're not going to try to take off on your own?"

Her mouth opened, closed, and opened again. Dropping her eyes, because she couldn't stand to look at him, she said, "No."

It was a lie, but only a partial one. She knew they were truemates, but she couldn't stay—not when she knew that the lynxes would never let her go and that the three males would most likely kill Bo right in front of her. It would destroy her. Even though it burned, she'd rather him live happily ever after with someone else than be killed fighting for her.

He said nothing and resumed his unpacking. She stewed in silence, cursing the well-crafted bed she was shackled to and the thick handcuff. But she didn't curse Bo. She knew he was going to do this exact thing—well, maybe not kidnap her—but she knew if he found out she was going to run away and hide to keep him and his pack safe, that he'd stop her. He was noble and loyal. He deserved a mate who came free of nasty attachments like three lynxes who wanted to breed her like a mare.

He brewed a pot of coffee and then joined her on the bed, sitting next to her hip. He set a steaming cup of coffee on the small side table and held a small bowl of cut fruit in his other hand. He lifted a section of peeled apple and held it to her lips. "Come on, sweetheart. Be mad all you like, but don't starve yourself."

She reached for the apple and he moved away slightly, "I'll feed you, Reika."

"I'm not entirely helpless." She snorted.

One brow rose slightly. "I never said you were. But we're mates, and mates take care of each other in all ways."

He waited patiently, moving the apple close to her mouth again. The smell of the apple made her stomach growl. She opened her mouth, feeling like a petulant child, and he slipped half of it inside. The fruit crunched between her teeth, firm and sweet, and she chewed slowly and swallowed. He fed her in silence for several minutes—red seedless grapes, sliced apples, and sliced bananas—and gave her sips of coffee.

When the fruit was gone and the mug empty, he put the dishes on the table and cleared his throat. "Here's the deal, sweetheart. I know what's going on in that pretty little head of yours. You think by taking off that you're going to spare me or my pack from whatever those assholes will do to get you back. Well, I can promise you several things. First, there's no way in hell that would have ever worked." He leaned forward, bracing his hands on the headboard and dropping his head to the crux of her neck. With a slow, deep inhale that made her nerve endings go haywire, he growled, "I would find you wherever you went. There isn't a place on this earth where you can hide from me, so toss that thought out of your mind for good.

"Second, I will fight for you and break whatever promise your alpha made to those assholes. You were a child. It was cruel and unfair, not to mention sick. As your truemate, I demand the right to fight to break your promise. And lastly, baby, listen very carefully. You're mine and that makes you part of my pack. My alpha, his mate, and my brothers and sisters in the pack are all supporting us. Jason won't sell you down the river to make peace, and I will do anything—any-fucking-thing—to keep you safe. I would go to the grave for you in a heartbeat. But don't worry. I don't plan to lose because I've got a lifetime of making sweet love to you to look forward to."

"I don't want you to die," she croaked, her voice cracking as tears clouded her vision.

"I won't. I might get beat all to hell, but I'm not going to leave you. Not now, not ever."

He nipped at her neck, licked the light mark he made, and then sat back. "We're only an hour and a half from your home pack. This place belongs to a rogue wolf, a friend of my mother's. They used to use it back in the day when wolves owned cattle farms and didn't want to risk killing their stock on the full moons. They would shift down here and take out their aggression on a side of beef instead. So the walls are soundproof, and no one can find us here."

She stared at him in disbelief. "But they'll tear your town apart looking for me, especially if they think I've left."

"I've got that all handled, baby. Jason called your alpha, and he contacted the lynx king who agreed to pull his grandsons back home. We're going to show up in neutral territory on Saturday. Your pack, my pack, and the lynx clan. I'll fight for you, win, and then you can thank me with your body, later." He grinned. It all seemed so casual for him. As if he weren't going to face off with three psycho males who had spent the better part of sixteen years waiting for her.

"You've just got it all figured out, don't you?" She was really feeling petulant now.

"Yes, I do, baby. Now, are you ready to admit what you're feeling for me or do I need to convince you of how perfect we are together?"

"Let me go."

He hummed in his throat and reached for the blanket wrapped around her. "Wrong answer."

She pushed at his hands with her free hand, but he simply pinned her wrist to the bed and used his other hand to open the blanket and bare her body to him. He leaned forward to kiss her and before she could protest or turn away, his mouth had claimed hers and all rational thought flew out of her mind. She loved his mouth. The way his stubble grazed her skin, the slick heat of his mouth, and his talented tongue that danced against hers. She knew he was trying to seduce her into promising to stay, and she knew that she should protest what he was doing, but her betraying body wanted her to do nothing of the sort.

Heat flashed through her, and she relaxed under him, making a small noise in her throat as he sat back on his heels next to her. He didn't ask her if she was ready to give in yet, and she didn't say she was. She didn't say anything at all as he pulled his shirt off and tossed it away before moving to stand on the floor and remove his jeans. He held her gaze without fear this time, as he kicked off his boots and shoved his jeans down his legs. He touched the healing marks on his leg almost reverently and said with a rough voice, "Before you healed me, I had already decided I wasn't going to ever let you go. Bum leg and all, I would have fought to break your vow. But you gave me back my life and my wolf, Reika. I want to give you back your life, too. We're truemates, and if it takes every second of these five days we have together to prove to you that you can trust me to keep you safe and set you free, then I'm going to do it."

He stepped free of his clothes and knelt on the bed between her legs. Warm fingers tickled their way up the insides of her legs, from the arch of her feet to the apex of her thighs, upwards to circle around her hipbones where sensitive skin was stretched taut, and then up the curve of her waist. Her skin tingled as he touched her, the look on his face telling her that he thought she was the most precious thing he'd ever seen.

His fingers slipped up the center of her body between her breasts and traced the contour of her collarbone before sliding through her hair and holding her still as his mouth descended on hers once more. Her stomach fluttered as he kissed her, and her free hand gripped him, digging into his flesh with her nails with each pleasurable stroke of his tongue against hers. She wound her legs around his waist, and he settled lower on her, his cock resting just above her pussy, where a few slight thrusts of his hips ground his rigid length against her swollen clit.

She moaned into his mouth, and he swallowed the sound, tilting his head further to deepen the kiss. Her body throbbed and her mind spun uselessly. He kissed across her cheek to her ear, where he traced the curve with his tongue, his hot breath washing over her skin.

"So fucking gorgeous," he whispered before kissing down her neck to her shoulder. His hands cupped her breasts, his rough thumbs teased her already hard nipples, alternating between circling them and pressing them between his thumb and forefinger. Each mild pinch made her breath catch, the ache blooming into pleasurable tingling. Lifting one breast, he lowered his head and darted his tongue across the pointed tip. He swiped his tongue across the other nipple before sucking it deep into his mouth with torturously slow pressure. Arching her back, she fisted her hand in his hair and said his name on a shaky breath.

Moving between her breasts, he licked and sucked the nipples until they were hot, tingling tips, dark and aching from his mouth and hands. His large hands moved down the curve of her waist as he pressed chaste kisses to each nipple and slipped down the bed. She mourned the loss of his weight and heat. He shoved her thighs roughly apart and slid his hands underneath to lift her lower body off the bed. For a brief moment, their eyes held, and she watched his hazel eyes darken as he probed her clit with his tongue.

Holding her body off the bed, he tilted his head and licked around the entrance to her body, delving his tongue into her hot core with fast strokes. Her legs fell wider, and she closed her eyes, surrendering to the sensations that coursed through her. Bo's fingers dug into her ass as he speared his tongue into her pussy, stroking the sensitive inner walls and scraping his stubble against her tender flesh. Her body wept, liquefying. One hand slipped forward, and his thumb replaced his tongue, pressing into her while his lips captured her swollen, sensitive clit.

He sucked her hard nub in a rhythm, gently then hard, slow then fast, fingers splayed on her ass and holding her up so he could feast on her. Her belly tightened and she took in a deep breath. His thumb moved out of her pussy and circled her arousal around her tightest place.

She felt his teeth graze her clit as his thumb breeched her, pushing inside while his tongue lashed her clit. Pressure built in her. His thumb pushed in all the way and he sucked her clit hard, fast, and deeply into his mouth and pulled his thumb out. As he plunged his thumb back into her, she came, her body exploding as she arched up with a cry of pleasure, her hips thrusting between his mouth and his thumb. Riding her pleasure, he thrust his thumb in and out of her body and licked her clit with hard, fast strokes. Her climax never ebbed, but rose higher and higher until she wailed his name and came a second time.

Writhing under him as he pulled his thumb from her completely, he moved over top of her, and caught her chin in his fingers.

"Are you mine yet, sweetheart?" he asked.

"Please, Bo, please," she moaned, wrapping her legs around his waist and pulling on him.

He groaned, seeming to struggle against his own control, and with a low, heavy sound, he thrust into her. Her hips met his again and again, as their bodies pressed together. She lifted one leg higher on his back and curled the other down lower on one leg, spreading her body slightly, digging her fingers into his shoulder. He swiveled his hips as he pounded into her, reaching a hand between them to finger her clit.

His rough finger flicked her tender clit in time to his cock thrusting into her hot, wet pussy. Her body clenched his again and again as he deviled her clit and dropped his head down to her shoulder, breathing hard. Her panting cries of pleasure drifted into one long moan as her body locked up in a spiral of pleasure and shuddered under him.

"Fuck, yes, fuck," Bo chanted, pounding into her with wild abandon, following her climax with his own as he rode out her pleasure and came with one final, hard thrust, burying himself inside her.

Settling his weight on his elbows, he kissed her, nuzzling her cheek and neck. "I love you so much, baby," Bo said with a rough voice. He moved off her, knelt in front of his jeans and searched the front pockets. He stood with a small key and unlocked her wrist from the cuff.

He put the key on the small side table and went to a cooler and brought back two bottles of water. As he sat next to her and handed her a bottle of water, he said, "I know you didn't promise yet."

She took a long drink, leaning her head back against the pillow and closing her eyes. "You're asking me to be okay with you putting your life on the line for me, Bo. I never will be."

"You want to be with another wolf?"

Her eyes popped open. "What? Of course not."

His eyes narrowed. "You want me fucking another she-wolf?" He stroked his hand across her belly. "You want another she-wolf to carry my children?"

She took in a slow breath as a riot of emotions coursed over her at the thought of his hands touching anyone but her. Of his mouth kissing another woman.

She steeled herself. Reminded her jealous wolf that staying with him could very well mean his death.

Placing the water bottle on the side table, she rolled to her side away from him and covered herself with a blanket. She felt his eyes on her, but she refused to give in. Admitting that she was his and he was hers … it just wasn't something she was willing to do, even if knowing that he would find another female eventually was like a fiery blade in her heart.

That's how the next few days went. They talked. He made her meals, and they ate together. And in between the mundane stuff, he blew her mind with screaming, hot sex. Against the wall. On the stairs. In the tiny bathroom. Every time he asked her to promise to stay, she refused, biting her tongue to keep from swearing a vow in her passion. But he was steadily wearing away at her defenses while their time together wound down.

Bo was stretched out next to her on the bed, eyes closed in sleep and a peaceful expression on his face. A glance at the clock on the wall told her it was nearly eleven on Thursday, their third night in the cellar of the barn. In one of their many talks, he had told her that they were supposed to meet her pack and the lynxes at three p.m. on Saturday. Earlier that evening, as they'd made love, she'd stared into his passion-filled gaze and knew that whether she promised to stick with him or not, he was going to fight for her. He would handcuff her again, haul her around like a ragdoll, and go to battle for her blood-debt. She'd come to understand that her refusal to accept his willingness to fight for her was hurting him. Not physically, of course, but emotionally. Here was a man who was walking right into hell for her without a second thought, and continuing to refuse his decision made a mockery of their bond.

Her fingertips ghosted over the marks on his shoulder where her jaws had snapped down hard and deep to force the healing venom into his body. They lingered, a reminder that even if the human part of her had refused to acknowledge that they were truemates, her wolf-self had known all along.

Fear lodged in her throat like a tight fist as she snuggled into him, curving her leg around his hip and sliding her hand up his smooth back. She couldn't hold back her feelings any longer, and if he wanted her support, if he wanted her vow that she would stand beside him, trust him, to fight for her, then she would give it. Willingly.

"Bo?" She nuzzled his chin and scratched her fingernails lightly across his back. "Bo, wake up. I need you."

His arms tightened around her, and his eyes opened slowly. "Are you alright, sweetheart?"

She ignored her worry for his safety, shoved the dark thoughts away, and opened her heart. "I love you."

His eyes widened, and his brows lifted for a brief moment before he rolled over top of her and grinned. "I love you, too."

She wiggled under him. "Make love to me."

Her legs parted, and he slipped into the cradle of her body, his cock hardening as their mouths met in a deep kiss. His tongue tangled with hers, dancing and touching every inch. Their hands clasped together, and he rose above her, thrusting into her with one hard press until their bodies were wed together as tightly as possible. Squeezing his hands, she locked her ankles in the small of his back and met his pounding thrusts with her own. Their bodies sang together, a song of bliss and love and passion that made lights wink behind her eyes and her heart pound in her chest.

As pleasure poured over her, the words on her lips were the truest she'd ever spoken.

"I'll never leave you, I swear!"

Chapter Eleven

Bo didn't think success had ever been so sweet. Here was his sweetheart, his *mate*, writhing under him in ecstasy, as she promised she'd never leave.

The tight heaven of her body locked down on him, and he came hard, pumping deep into her. He let go of her hands and gathered her close, kissing her as she panted for breath and shivered.

Her arms wrapped around him, and she whispered, "Mark me, Bo, and make me yours forever."

The happy growl rumbled from his chest as he kissed her once and tilted her head. Their kind normally marked at the back of the neck, directly over the spine, but Bo wanted her marks visible to everyone. While she still shuddered from her post-orgasmic bliss, he sank his teeth into the side of her neck.

"Oh," she moaned, wiggling under him and scraping her nails down his sides. She shifted her head slightly and sank her own fangs down into the side of his neck. His whole body shuddered as they held each other captive. He'd never known fangs could be so erotic, but damn if he didn't want her to bite him more often.

Extracting her fangs, she said with a sex-roughened voice, "If you die on me, I'm going to be so pissed." She licked across the marks and growled softly. Extracting his fangs from her neck, he caught her blood on his tongue and sighed happily.

"I have no intention of dying, sweetheart."

She brushed the back of her hand across his cheek. Now that her guard was down, he could see the love she had for him clearly, could feel their wolves communing together in the way that only truemates could. For the rest of their lives, he would be able to find her wherever she was, and now that his leg was healed, he could protect her not only in his human form, but also his wolf form.

"There are three of them." She frowned, her brows drawing together. He kissed the corner of her mouth and rolled them both to their sides.

"Baby, please trust me. Trust me to keep you safe. Trust that I know what I'm doing. I don't take this lightly. If I thought for a moment that I might lose, I would take you so far away from here, bury us so deep, that they'd never find us."

He could see the war in her eyes and knew that she still battled with her desire to see him safe. Wolf mates shared protective feelings for each other equally. His need to protect her was equal to her need to protect him. He knew that humans didn't always understand that. They often viewed the males as having all the power, all the protective instincts. But a she-wolf was a beautiful and deadly force of nature. He'd seen Reika fight off those three lynxes, and even though she lost that battle, she had been as determined and as fierce as any she-wolf he'd ever known. And her healing abilities just made her that much more unique and powerful in his mind.

"I do trust you, Bo. I do." She closed her eyes and pressed her forehead against his. "I do."

He fingered the already healing marks on her neck. "You're mine now, Reika. As long as there is breath in my body, no one will ever touch you again."

She kissed him and they made love once more, slowly this time, so he could savor everything about her.

Her eyes were half-lidded, her hair mussed, and her lips swollen from kissing. Her skin was flushed and dewy, and the scent of her was like a drug he couldn't get enough of.

He'd kept her locked up for three days. She was one stubborn she-wolf. It had been hard for him to see her fight her true feelings in the name of protecting him and his pack. He knew she would fit right into the Tressel Pack because she already cared so much for them.

He opened his mouth to ask her if she was hungry and found her asleep, her hands tucked under her cheek. Exiting the bed slowly so he didn't wake her, he checked his messages and sent a few texts to the pack before tucking it away and crawling into bed with his mate.

When he woke late the next the morning, the bed beside him was cold. His heart leapt into his throat as he jumped from the bed, worried she'd found a way to get out. The bathroom door opened, and she walked out, wearing one of his T-shirts. "You look like you saw a ghost." She laughed, kissing his cheek.

He swallowed hard, ashamed that his first thought had been that she'd tried to leave him after promising she wouldn't. "We've got one more day together, baby, and since we're newly mated, I wanted to make sure we started the day right."

"Aw." She kissed his nose. "I'm starving. Someone put me in another sex coma last night."

"I can't help it. I can't get enough of your hot body." He nipped her ear, and she giggled.

They made breakfast together, watched a movie on his iPad, and talked. He learned so much about her in those few days in the cellar. Not only confirming what he already knew, that she was smart and caring and an all around amazing person, but that she was also incredibly sweet and nurturing. He felt like he was basking in the sun when he was around her.

That night, they made love and fell asleep in each other's arms. He wanted to spend every night that way and wake up every morning with her being the first thing he saw.

As they packed up to head to her home pack on Saturday, he felt her anxiety grow with each minute that passed. By the time he unlocked the cellar door and opened the hatch, she was trembling with nerves. "Baby, it'll be okay, I promise," he swore, cupping her face and kissing her lips.

"I know that in my heart, Bo, but I'm so afraid to lose you." She squeezed her hands into tight fists as if to control her trembling, but they still shook visibly when she released them.

"You won't." He raised her palms to his mouth and kissed the center of each one before pulling her into a hug and holding her close.

He put her in the truck along with their supplies and opened the doors of the barn wide. When he backed the truck out and turned around, Reika gasped. Ten vehicles were in a long line in front of the barn.

She peered through the windshield. "Is that your pack?"

He squeezed her hand. "They're your pack now, too, sweetheart. Don't forget that. They came here to support us. Nothing is more important to a wolf than his truemate, and a pack that would let a wolf stand alone is no wolf pack I'd ever be part of."

She turned to face him, her eyes bright with unshed tears. "I love you," she whispered thickly.

"I love you, too, sweetheart."

He pulled around the line of vehicles and horns blared, breaking the morning silence. Leading the way, he pulled out of the long drive of the farm and headed towards Columbus, where three lynxes were about to get a lesson … old-school.

"Oh, Mom!" Reika cried as she closed the distance to a woman who looked like a slightly older version of her. The woman hugged Reika tightly, and the two started to cry. Grim, the alpha of their pack, stepped forward and met with Jason, and they shook hands. Reika's father, Tin, shook Jason's hand and then Bo's.

"Welcome to the family, son," Tin said with a nod. "You have no idea how long we have prayed that the great wolf spirit would allow her to find her truemate."

"I'm not going to let her down," Bo promised.

Tin smiled, briefly, and introduced Ben. Ben was a few inches shorter than Bo's six feet, stocky and well muscled. Reika had painted him as a chef, and Bo had pictured him being thin and geeky. He might like to cook, but he was packing some serious muscle.

A strange sound, like a bullhorn, echoed around the empty park. It was neutral territory west of the city of Columbus, a wide open grassy park, lined with trees. The lynx clan appeared in a huge caravan of RVs. They circled the RVs around the perimeter of the park, and Bo was reminded of when wagons would circle up in the old west. It was strange, to say the least.

They were like a swarm as they stepped out of the RVs. There had to be a hundred and fifty of them who stood around the clearing. A grizzled old male stepped forward with the three males who had been promised Reika.

The lynxes joined Alpha Grim, Jason, and Bo in the center of the clearing, with the wolves from both Bo's and Reika's packs standing to the side while the lynxes crowded around the open space.

"King Maurice," Alpha Grim said, "I present to you Bo Elliot, werewolf truemate to Reika Snow. By our laws *and* yours, a truemate can break the blood-debt promise."

The three males growled in anger, their eyes narrowing. Maurice raised his wrinkled hand, and the males stopped growling.

"We have waited sixteen years for the healer to join our clan. If he is truly her truemate, then he will have to fight those who hold the blood-debt. Only blood can erase the blood-debt."

The crowd pushed back, urged by Alpha Grim, until only Bo stood in the clearing with the four lynxes. Bo held his hand out to Reika, and she walked to him quickly. He took off his leather jacket and handed it to her. She slipped it on her shoulders, and he reached over and touched the marks on her neck. Without looking at the males, he said with a loud, clear voice, "I, Bo Elliot, do hereby declare myself champion to my truemate, Reika Snow. I will take on her blood-debt as my own."

A tear trickled down her cheek. "I love you," she murmured.

He kissed her and repeated the words back to her.

And here was his ace in the hole.

"I call two *fregoris* to fight by my side in blood and honor."

The lynxes around them erupted in unhappy murmurs.

Ben and Shayne stepped from the wolves and came to stand on either side of Bo. The lynx males paled when they saw Shayne, and Bo relished their reaction. Shayne and his family had traveled with their pack to support Bo.

"What is the meaning of this?" Maurice shrieked.

Grim and Jason came to stand with them. Grim spoke loudly, authority in every word. "In your own laws, it is stated that a male may ask for warriors to fight with him, but only if those warriors have been wronged by the same men. You hurt Ben's sister, Reika, when you attacked her in your shifted forms when she ran. And you injured Shayne's sister, Jazlyn, when you tried to use her as collateral to force Bo to release Reika."

Jason said, "You may take the three wolves in challenge to your three lynxes, or you may choose one to battle Bo alone. It is not honorable to demand an uneven fight."

"You know nothing of us or our laws," one of the grandsons snarled.

"Fight or walk away," Grim said, "but this ends today."

Bo glanced towards Reika and saw her staring at him in shock. He'd been willing to go against all three males, but when Alpha Grim told Jason about the lynx laws, Bo knew that there was nothing better in a fight than two wolves at his back. He hadn't known much about Ben, but when Jason talked to Grim about the situation, he assured Jason that Ben was a serious fighter and would happily fight for his sister's honor.

The lynx males pulled off their jackets, cursing under their breaths, and stalked forward. "Flesh to flesh. If you shift, you are disqualified from the fight," Alpha Grim said.

Shayne cracked his neck, his bright blue eyes flashing as he sought out the male who had put his hands on Jazlyn. Shayne was 280 pounds of pure, primal male. The lynx didn't stand a chance.

The onlookers moved back further to give the fighters more room, as each male chose an opponent. Bo knew he was looking at Eli, the eldest.

The three wolves faced off against the three lynxes. The onlookers had given them a wide berth, and Bo focused all his attention on Eli, his vision narrowing on the male who had been a threatening presence for almost Reika's entire life.

Bo's wolf was anxious to end the threat to his mate, and for the first time, he felt truly at one with his beast. The only thing standing in the way of his utter happiness was one pathetic excuse for a male. Bo waited for him to make the first move, guessing he would try to disable him quickly, choosing brute strength over strategy. Eli was bigger than Bo, but Bo knew he could beat Eli.

As he suspected, Eli rushed him with a roar, and Bo grappled him as the two landed hard on the ground. He was only very dimly aware of the sounds of Ben and Shayne fighting, but he pushed the thoughts away. He couldn't lose focus now, not when Reika's welfare depended on it.

She was the most incredible woman he'd ever known, and she belonged to him now, as his mate, his equal, and his future wife. There was no way in hell he was going to lose the most important thing he'd ever stood up for in his life.

Chapter Twelve

Reika stifled a cry of alarm as Eli threw himself at Bo and landed on top of him, the two hitting the ground with a loud thud. She was aware of her brother and Shayne fighting the other lynx males, but her vision had narrowed down to Bo and his fight. She'd been so surprised her mate had found a way to make the fight even. She had said she trusted him, and she did, but she hadn't been certain what the outcome would be if he had to face all three. Her mate was determined, though.

Within seconds, the two were apart again, Bo looking calm and in control and Eli looking like a wild man. They circled for a few moments, gauging each other, and this time when Eli moved to strike, Bo hit first. For each punch and kick that Eli threw, Bo returned ten, his fists and feet moving so fast that she could barely track the movements with her eyes.

Eli landed a solid punch to Bo's right eye, and Reika felt her mother's restraining hand on her arm, not realizing she had taken a step forward. Her breath caught in her throat at the sight of her mate's blood, and her wolf growled in worry in her mind.

Eli landed a hard kick to what had once been Bo's bad leg, and Bo went to the ground with a grunt. Reika nearly screamed in panic, wanting to throw herself between Eli and Bo as Eli reached for her mate with pure menace and hatred in his eyes. Bo kicked out suddenly and swept Eli off his feet. Eli hit the ground so hard that Reika thought she could actually hear his brain rattle around his skull.

Bo twisted Eli around until Eli's arms were braced behind his back by one arm and Bo's other arm was wrapped tightly around

Eli's neck. Eli struggled, arching against Bo to try to free himself, kicking vainly at the ground. His face began to darken as Bo cut off his oxygen. The muscles in Bo's arm tensed as he squeezed tighter, and Eli's struggles slowed and then stopped.

Bo dropped Eli's unconscious body to the ground and stood up, lifting his head to the sky and howling in victory. Ben and Shayne stood victorious over the unconscious bodies of the other lynx males, joining Bo in their shared victory. The wolves around them erupted in a chorus of answering howls, and Reika raised her head and let loose a howl in thanks to the great wolf spirit for seeing her mate safe and for erasing the blood-debt against her.

Bo lowered his head and glared at the lynx clan leader. Maurice lifted a thin dagger from his belt and sliced across his palm. When several drops of blood had splashed onto the grass, he said, "The blood-debt is answered, the she-wolf Reika Snow is free."

Reika's heart soared. Free! Free to love who she wanted, no longer looking over her shoulder.

Maurice spoke several words in a language she didn't know, spat, and tossed the blade into the ground with an angry snort. He turned his back and stalked away towards the RVs, snapping his fingers and barking orders at his people. The three unconscious lynxes were picked up by their people and carried off.

Bo swept his eyes over the crowd and met her eyes as tears of relief and happiness streaked down her face. He opened his arms to her, and she raced forward and clung to him as he wrapped his arms around her while she sobbed.

"I'm okay, sweetheart," he said, hushing her gently, stroking her hair with one hand and holding her close with the other.

She cried harder, unable to contain the tears any longer, and he stood with her until she'd cried all that she could. "Thank you, thank you," she said with a rough voice, squeezing her arms around him.

"I promised it would be okay, didn't I?" he asked when she lifted her face to look at him. She sniffled and nodded.

"I love you so much, sweetheart. I would gladly have died to see you free and safe." She shivered at the statement, even though she knew that she, too, would die for him. He stroked the back of his hand over her cheek. "I didn't know what real love was until I met you, sweetheart. Real love is wanting the person you love to be safe from all harm, even if it means dying to ensure it. Real love means being willing to be broken, battered, and bruised, if it means that the person you love won't be harmed. I love you that much. I truly do."

"I love you, too, Bo. My protector. My heart."

"Your mate," he added.

Reika wiped at the tears under her eyes and stepped back from him, looking him over with a critical eye. A bruise was already forming around one eye, and blood had dried under his nose and at one corner of his mouth, and she was certain he was bruised on his body, even though she couldn't see underneath the clothes.

She glanced at her brother and Shayne, who had fought beside Bo. She'd never been more proud of her brother or more grateful for the quiet man who stood off to the side of the group with his own pack. Taking Bo's hand, she walked over to her brother, who was being looked over by the sharp eyes of her mother. "Thank you, Ben," she said and hugged him gingerly, worried he was more injured than he appeared.

Ben hugged her back. "I wanted to make it right, Kiki. It was my foolishness that caused it to happen in the first place."

"No," their father said, "you were just being a child. It was an accident with severely unfortunate consequences, but we can put it behind us now."

She hugged her mom and dad and then pulled Bo over to Shayne. She had heard Bo mention the man who was part of a small pack that lived outside Allen. Touching Shayne's large hand, she looked up into his eyes and said, "You're an honorable man, Shayne. Thank you for standing with Bo to help set me free."

His brows rose in surprise, and he ducked his head in a nod, saying with a deep voice, "It was my honor, Reika, to stand with a male such as your mate."

She looked at the members of Shayne's pack—his family—and smiled at them gratefully. "Thank you."

Jazlyn stepped from the embrace of a young wolf who Bo identified as her mate, Fritz, and hugged Reika. "Your mate stood up for me. There was no way that we were going to let him stand alone. We are not of the same pack, but we're sisters in wolf-nature, and that can be as strong as family lines. Stronger, sometimes."

"It's my honor to call you sister, Jazlyn." Reika hugged the petite she-wolf back and then let Bo pull her away as he thanked Shayne and his pack and turned to go back to Reika's family and his pack.

Reika looked over her shoulder and said, "I should offer to heal him if he's injured."

Bo chuckled. "I'm pretty sure he'd rather just shift than suffer through your biting."

She shook her head. "I only bite for severe injuries like yours. For smaller things, I can just shift and lick the wound."

Bo pulled her to an abrupt stop and spun her close. "You will not lick any males but me, Reika."

Laughing, she said, "But I'm a healer. How am I supposed to heal people if I can't lick them?"

He seemed to consider what she said, and then he narrowed his hazel eyes at her and said, "I will insist on being there, then."

She teased, "You don't trust me?"

He jerked her against his body with a soft growl, his eyes flashing to amber for a moment. "I trust you with my life, sweetheart. I just don't trust anyone else."

She touched the cheek that wasn't bruised. "You gave me back my life, Bo. I hope you know that I'm yours forever."

"I wouldn't have it any other way." He lowered his mouth to hers and kissed her, just briefly. Her first kiss as a free woman.

Alpha Grim clapped his hands together and the wolves all quieted down. "Sixteen years ago, I was forced to make a choice between one young girl and a war. Although I hated it, the choice was made for the sake of the pack. In all these years, we held out hope that Reika's truemate would find her and break her blood-debt." He looked at her and Bo and then behind them at the members of the Tressel Pack who had gathered, and Shayne and his pack, as well.

"Thank you for your support, proving that a wolf is not bound by his or her packs, but instead by the bonds of friendship and love."

Reika's father said loudly, "Let's celebrate at the lodge!"

Her pack cheered and began to head to their vehicles. "What's the lodge?" Jason asked, coming to stand next to them.

"It's like a meeting hall. The pack gathers there for parties and meetings. It's near the alpha's house." She looked up at Bo. "We can stay, right?"

He looked surprised. "Of course, sweetheart. As long as you want."

"I want to visit with my family for a little while."

"I have it on good authority that your boss doesn't need you back at the shop until Wednesday, so you guys can stay here for a few days." Jason smiled.

"Thanks, Jason," Bo said, leaning to Jason as the two clapped each other on the back a few times and then separated quickly. She smiled at her mate and held his hand as they walked over to his truck. He took back his jacket before he sat down behind the wheel, and she leaned over and hooked her arm through his as he pulled into the long line of vehicles heading towards her pack's territory and the lodge.

When they walked through the double doors of the lodge, Bo made a surprised noise. She looked up at him and he shrugged, saying, "I'm just surprised they put something like this together so fast."

Her mom, who had come to greet them, laughed, "When Alpha Grim said what was happening today, that Reika's mate was going to fight for her blood-debt, the females in the pack decided to have a celebration meal ready for when the fight was over."

Bo hummed in his throat. "They had a lot of faith in me."

Her mom said, "We take truemates very seriously here, son."

They followed her mom to a large table towards the front of the room where Alpha Grim and his wife sat. Alpha Grim invited Jason and the rest of the wolves with him to join him at the head table, and Bo pulled Reika's chair out and pushed it in gently, before sitting next to her. Reika's mom disappeared into the large commercial kitchen, but she knew she'd be back to sit down and eat.

Jason sat next to Bo, followed by Michael, Linus, Logan, Teller, and Toby. Shayne and his family settled further down the table. Reika had just met Toby today and was told that he worked security at the bar and she could see why. He was a large man, towering well over six feet, with very broad shoulders and thick with muscles.

Her family joined the long table as the young wolves from her pack began to set huge bowls and platters overflowing with food on the tables. Like her own pack, the males in Bo's pack waited while the females filled their plates and then they fell on the food like locusts, laughter and chatter mingling as they ate.

"I packed up most of your clothes," her mother said, as Reika cut into a slice of honey glazed ham.

"Thanks, Mom."

Her mother looked up from her plate and smiled, her blue eyes crinkling. "I was happy to pack you up under these circumstances."

"Now we just have to get rid of the other one," her father said with a laugh.

"Oh thanks," Ben chuckled as he sat down across from Reika, after helping in the kitchen.

Lively conversation flowed around them as they ate, the young wolves refilling the bowls and platters when they were empty.

As the meal wound down, Linus leaned back in his chair and said, "That was the best barbecue pork I've ever had!"

Jason laughed and said, "Don't let Karly hear you say that."

Linus shrugged. "Hey, she's not so insecure that she can't admit when someone can cook something amazing. Who made it? Maybe they can give me the recipe to give to her."

Ben looked up. "It was me."

Bo said, "Reika said you could cook, but I had no idea how well. Did you make everything?"

Ben's cheeks tinted with a blush. Her mother rushed to answer, "He directed all of it. When the females decided we needed a community meal, Ben took over and prepared everything with help from the females and the young wolves. He really is fantastic."

He grinned under the flurry of compliments, and it filled Reika with joy to see her baby brother praised.

Dessert was served, a dozen different cakes and pies and plates of cookies, along with coffee, and slowly the members of her home pack began to clear out and head home.

She and Bo walked his pack members out to their vehicles and thanked them all once more for their support.

Jason said, "Next full moon, Reika can join the pack, and you can declare each other as mates at the same time, if you're ready."

Bo put his arm around her. "Oh, we're ready."

She heard running footsteps and turned to see Ben with a paper grocery sack in his hands. "Here," Ben said, handing it to Linus. "I put the recipe in there and some leftovers, too."

"Wow, thanks," Linus said and then lowered his voice slightly, speaking quietly to Ben.

She and Bo turned away from his pack members with a wave and headed to his truck to drive to her parent's home. They would be spending the next few days with her family, and she looked forward to Bo and her family getting to know each other.

As they drove away, she noticed that Ben was still talking to Bo's pack, and she made a mental note to ask him about it later.

When Bo carried the duffel bag up to her bedroom, she locked the door and pushed him to the bed.

"Really, sweetheart? Your parents are right downstairs," he teased, as she pulled his shoes off and straightened, reaching for the button of his jeans.

"Not for sex, Bo," she fussed, drawing his pants down his legs, "I want to see your injuries."

"I'm fine, love," he promised, but let her strip him anyway. She ran her fingers over every inch of his body, noticing the fading bruises and healing cut marks that had been the evidence of the brutal battle for her freedom.

She stretched out next to him. "Did I say thank you?"

"A man never tires of hearing his woman say thank you." He twined his hand with hers.

She smiled. "Thank you, Bo. For rescuing me in the woods, keeping me safe even against my own wishes, and most of all, for loving me enough to set me free."

He rolled to his side. "It was completely selfish."

"What was?"

"Setting you free. I wanted to keep you for myself forever."

"You can be selfish anytime."

"I'd like to be selfish right now and spend some quality naked time together."

He tugged her shirt from her jeans with a wicked smile and they made love, reveling in her freedom.

Spending time with her family without the threat of the lynxes filled her with a joy she hadn't known before. Ben made her a birthday cake, just as she'd requested, and this time as they sang to her and the twenty-three candles flickered on the cake, her heart wasn't filled with dread. Instead, she closed her eyes and wished for a happy life for her family, now that they, too, were free from the lynxes. She wasn't the only one who had been burdened by the blood-debt all those years. Even though she'd kept a brave face for so long, her family suffered right along with her. Her home pack seemed happier, too. Alpha Grim had stopped by on Monday night to wish her and Bo a safe journey back to Allen.

Alpha Grim also thanked Bo for breaking the vow and then asked Reika to forgive him. She looked up in wonder at the man who had represented supreme authority her whole life.

"There is nothing to forgive, Alpha Grim."

He pressed his lips together and then said, "I am grateful you feel that way, Reika, but I would still appreciate your forgiveness. That I wasn't able to get out of securing you in a blood-debt. That I couldn't find a way to break it once it was made."

She glanced at Bo, who nodded. All those years, she had never hated the alpha for what he had done. She had hated the lynxes for forcing his hand, but had never once thought any less of him. "I forgive you."

He smiled, picked up her hand, kissed the top, and ducked out the door without another word.

Tuesday afternoon, as Bo and her father were loading up Bo's truck to head back to Allen, Reika walked down the hall to Ben's room and knocked on the door. He looked up from his laptop and smiled.

"What's up, Sis?"

"I just wanted to say goodbye." She sat down on his bed and looked around his slightly messy room.

"Maybe not."

"Maybe not, what?" she asked, looking at him in confusion.

He turned the laptop around, and she saw his email program was open to an email from Karly Mayfield.

Ben, it's my pleasure to offer you the position of sous chef at Lonestar's. You'll work directly under me, helping to create the menu as we get ready to open the restaurant in time for our special Valentine's dinner. Once open, you'll be responsible for prep, working particular areas during service, and leading when I'm away. As discussed, your starting salary will be $25,000 annually with quarterly bonuses based on the restaurant's profits. I look forward to working with you. Karly

She met Ben's eyes over the lid of the laptop. "You're moving to Allen?"

"Yeah. When I gave Linus the barbecue leftovers, he said that his wife Karly would probably want to talk to me some on the phone once she tasted the food. Then Jason said that if things worked out, I could join their pack and work for Karly at the restaurant."

He beamed at her while her mouth hung open in surprise. "Do Mom and Dad know?"

"Sure, Sis. I told them about it that night, and they said they're glad to see me use my talents finally working some place worthwhile. I get to help build the restaurant from the ground up, and Karly has got some really great ideas."

"Where will you live?"

He quirked his head to the side. "I can't live with my sister and her new mate?"

She snapped her teeth together and felt her eyes widen at the thought of letting him room in her new home. He started snickering, and she narrowed her eyes at him.

He rolled his eyes with a smile. "I was just kidding, but thanks for the vote of confidence. Jason said that one of their wolves just moved away, and he had a small house that he rented out to a few wolves my age. It's four bedrooms, and there are three guys in there now. He said I could join them until I make enough to get a place of my own."

She was simply stunned. But really happy. She put the laptop on the bed and gave him a big hug. "If you're happy, I'm happy."

"Good. I'm thrilled. I know my mate's not here in our pack, and I'm ready to branch out and make my own way."

She ruffled his dark hair. "You're too young to be thinking about finding a mate."

"I'm only three years younger than you," he chastised her as she stood and walked to the door.

"I know, but you'll always be my little brother."

A smile lit his face, and his dark blue eyes twinkled. "Love you, Kiki."

"Love you."

As they headed back to Allen on Tuesday night, she and Bo talked about her and Ben joining the pack, their mating announcement, and what she was going to do now that she was free of the pall of the lynxes.

Ever since that fateful day, she had felt like it didn't matter what plans she made for herself because they were going to take her away and keep her prisoner. Going to college had felt futile, but she'd gone to make her parents happy. They had hoped, and she had, too, that she would find her truemate somewhere on campus, or really at any place between age seven and her twenty-third birthday. But it hadn't happened, and she'd taken to the road instead. That one foolish act of running for the hills had landed her right in Bo's arms, and although there were things she regretted in the past, she never regretted the actions that led her straight to him.

"What are you thinking about so seriously?" Bo tweaked a lock of her hair, and she turned from looking out the window to face him.

"That I love you."

His lips split into a wide grin. "I love you, too."

Chapter Thirteen

Wednesday morning, Bo left Reika at home and headed into work. He knew the threat of the lynxes was long gone, and he had it on good authority from Reika's home pack that the lynxes were already several states west of Ohio by the time he and Reika returned to Allen, and all he could think was *good riddance.*

It had been a surprise that her brother Ben was coming to join the pack, and Bo looked forward to getting to know the young male. He had moved into the home that once belonged to Clay, who was ranked fifth in the pack before he moved out of state with his human girlfriend. Ben was joining three other young wolves—Paul, Drake, and Luka—in the house, and Bo imagined that the single she-wolves in the pack would be very happy to have four single males in one place.

"Glad to see you back," Jason said, when Bo stopped in his office to check in.

"Thanks. It's good to be back home."

"I'll bet." Jason held out a work order, and Bo took it. "It's a renovation on a 1970 Mustang. Take a look and let me know your time and cost estimates, and I'll call the customer."

"Sounds good." Bo turned to leave and then stopped. "I don't know if I said thanks, Jason, but really, thank you for everything. I have my mate now because of the support of the pack."

Jason smiled. "You were there for me when we had to hunt down the wolves who kidnapped Cades, and you were also there for Linus when we couldn't find Karly after she was taken. We're family because we're a pack."

Nodding, Bo left Jason's office and headed into the bay to look at his new project.

A few hours later, as he dropped off his estimate to Jason and grabbed a bite to eat with Michael and Linus, Michael said that Reika had called Susan and accepted the part-time job at the community center and then had called Shyne to ask for a ride.

"She doesn't have a car?" Linus asked in surprise.

"She and Ben shared a car, and she wanted him to have it. Her dad offered to buy her a new car, but I said I'd take care of it. I thought I'd take her out this weekend to go car shopping. Does Shyne mind driving her this week?"

"Nah," Michael smiled, popping a chip into his mouth. "You know how women are. Shyne's a giggling chatterbox whenever another woman is nearby, and she really likes Reika."

Bo knew that Reika liked the women she'd met, but she'd hadn't really made any real connections with them because she'd had one eye trained on the door to escape. Now that she was staying with him forever, she could let go of her worries and have the friends that she'd been denied because of the blood-debt.

Aunt Lia stopped in for dinner that night and brought over a big container of her beef stew and fresh, crusty rolls. Reika and Lia talked about healing, and Bo was impressed with Reika's knowledge of herbal medicine.

She shrugged with a smile. "There are a lot of wolves, especially older ones, who prefer to use herbal medicine for aches and pains, and a good healer knows many forms of healing so she can best help her patients."

"Reika has agreed to help me with patients if I need it, and I'm sure a lot of wolves are going to be thrilled to have an apex in the pack now." Lia smiled, and her eyes crinkled.

Bo narrowed his eyes at Reika. "Remember what I said about licking males."

Reika burst out laughing and shook her head, filling Lia in on Bo's little jealousy issue.

Little jealousy issue?

He arched a brow, silently promising to get her back for that statement.

When Lia left for the night, Bo locked the front door and turned to face Reika as she stood from the couch and stretched. He watched her top lift slightly with the motion, and his cock hardened at the small bit of her flat belly that peeked out between her tight jeans and her shirt.

Snapping out of the trance her beauty sent him into, he stalked over to her and tossed her over his shoulder, stomping into the bedroom and kicking the door shut.

She laughed, her hands gripping his ass before he flipped her around and dropped her belly first onto the bed. Jerking her hips, he pulled until her feet were on the floor and her upper body was flat on the bed.

"I don't have a jealousy issue," he growled, trying to be stern when he felt incredibly giddy just to have her in his bed again.

Peeking over her shoulder, she bit her bottom lip and smiled slowly. "Yeah, you do."

He snarled, knowing she was baiting him. Leaning over, he licked the shell of her ear and said, "I'm not jealous. I'm protecting my woman. You *are* mine, aren't you, Reika?"

He licked the space behind her ear where her intoxicating scent lay heaviest, and she shivered and moaned, "Yes."

His wolf howled in his mind, and his human side grinned like an idiot to know that she really was his. He'd believed her before, but he could hear her say it a hundred times a day and never get tired of it.

Grasping either side of the collar of her shirt, he ripped it apart, seams tearing and buttons flying as he shoved it down to her elbows with her bra straps, until her breasts popped free. He nuzzled her ear as he slid his hands up, rubbing his fingers under the sensitive underside of her breasts before covering both swells with his hands and squeezing gently. Her nipples tightened and brushed against his palms as he pressed open mouthed kisses down her neck to the crux of her shoulder.

He felt her hands sink into his hair as she moaned, and he pulled her hands away and pressed them into the mattress. "Don't move your hands."

He paused for a moment to see if she would move, but she remained still. Until she wiggled her butt against him. "Are you going to just look at me or what?"

He swatted her ass lightly, and she squeaked in surprise, and then laughed, tossing her hair back and giving him a come-fuck-me look that almost melted his shoes off.

Unsnapping her jeans, he lowered the zipper and hooked his thumbs into the waistband of both her jeans and her panties and pushed them down her shapely legs and tossed them across the room. His fingers trailed up the backs of her legs, curving around the smooth line of her hips. She was so beautiful.

He stripped quickly, his shoes thudding against the far wall and his phone tumbling to the floor in his haste. Leaning forward, he swept her hair off her back and kissed the space between her shoulders. She lay flat on the bed, her arms out to the sides and her cheek resting on the comforter. He kissed down her back, delving his hands down her sides to her hips and hooking them around her legs to pull them apart.

Sliding his hands up the inside of her thighs, he skimmed the lips of her pussy and grinned at how turned on she was. He kissed her shoulder, biting down enough to leave a slight mark.

He straightened and picked up one of her legs at the knee and hooked it over his elbow, planting his hand on the bed to keep her body spread wide in front of him. With his other hand, he guided his cock into her heated core, groaning as she tightened around him.

Stroking out of her slowly, he grabbed her waist with his free hand and gripped the bed tighter with his other hand, before thrusting hard and fast into her. Her pussy was incredibly tight with her lower body spread the way it was, and he struggled to regain control of his body so he didn't come before she did.

Inching his hand around the front of her body, he rubbed her slick, swollen clit with one finger, growling as her body began to tighten rhythmically. She moaned and panted, her knuckles turning white where she gripped the comforter, while he strummed her clit and pounded into her.

She hunched forward and screamed his name as her pussy clamped down on his cock so hard his eyes crossed. His control snapped, and he rammed into her, clenching her tightly and pumping hard and fast into her body.

He felt his fangs elongate and claws break from the tips of his fingers as he came, and he jerked his hands away from her body and gripped the bed instead, howling his pleasure as his cock spasmed inside her. His nails dug into the comforter, tearing the fabric, as he let out a panting growl, his whole body shivering as the last of his come bathed her womb.

His fangs and claws receded quickly as his heartbeat slowed. He pulled out of the tight, wet heaven of her body and scooped her up into his arms and carried her onto the bed. He stretched out on his side and curled her into him. She snuggled close and hummed in her throat.

She lifted her head and blinked bright, happy eyes at him. "I love you."

He grinned. "I love you, too."

Dropping her head with a yawn, she cuddled closer and whispered, "Even if you are jealous."

"I heard that."

Bo hadn't ever given much though to Valentine's Day as anything other than a clever marketing ploy by greeting card companies and chocolatiers to hock their wares on unsuspecting idiots who didn't know any better. Now, of course, he could count himself among the idiots because he was going *all* out for Reika this year, starting with a reservation at Lonestar's for Karly's special, reservation-only, Valentine's Dinner. Doors opened at eight, and a four-course meal would be served.

Jason had asked Bo to double-date, and Bo had cleared it with Reika. He was pleased she was excited to get to know his best friend and Cades better.

As he showered after work that night, he mentally went over everything he had prepared. He had planned to just do the special dinner, but she told him that she'd never had a valentine before, which prompted him to do all the sappy, romantic stuff he had at one time teased his friends about.

Card? Check.

Flowers? Check.

Chocolate? Check.

He heard the front door shut and knew that Reika was home from her afternoon spent at the community center. She was working a few days a week and really enjoying herself. He was glad to see her coming out of her shell and embracing his pack.

"Bo?" she called, coming into the bedroom. He shut off the shower and reached for his towel.

"In here, baby."

The door opened, and she stuck her head in. "Did you have a nice day?"

"I did. You?"

"You bet. Now get out of the shower so I can clean up."

"Yes, ma'am."

He shaved while she showered, and when he rinsed his face off, she turned off the shower and dried off. He walked to the closet to get his freshly dry-cleaned slacks and dress shirt. When he heard the hair dryer click on, he rushed to finish getting dressed so he could get her gifts ready.

Thirty minutes later, when he was leaning against the counter and playing a game of poker on his cell, he heard the click of heels on the kitchen tile and lifted his head. His breath caught in his throat as she neared him and he took in her stunning beauty.

Her long black hair was swept to the right side of her neck in a long ponytail, which left his marks exposed on her neck and filled him with pride. She wore a glittering black jacket over a dark red dress that fell to her ankles and split up one leg to her knee. Her blue eyes looked darker and more luminous, a trick of makeup perhaps, or maybe she was just that happy.

"You look gorgeous, baby," he promised, closing the distance between them and pressing a kiss to her cheek.

"Thank you." She brushed her fingers along his smooth jaw and said, "You clean up really well, but I like the stubble, too."

"Do you?" He arched a brow at her.

She hummed in her throat. "When you go down on me, the stubble rubs on my thighs and I can … feel you … for hours afterwards. It's pretty cool."

And sexy, too.

"I'll remember that."

She tugged on his tie with a sweet smile. He turned and walked into the kitchen and brought out the vase of flowers he had purchased for her. Her eyes widened as he set it down on the counter. The crystal vase overflowed with two dozen red and dark pink roses mixed with pink and white lilies.

He handed her the simple card he had picked out at the florist. She opened it and read the words out loud: *To my Reika, I love you more than I ever believed possible. Forever, Bo*

After closing the card, she laid it on the counter next to the flowers and slipped her arms around him. Tipping her head back so she could look at him, she smiled, "That's the most romantic thing anyone has ever said to me, Bo Elliot."

He tried not to grin like an idiot, but in his head he was yelling, "Fuck yeah!" and throwing his fists in the air.

"It's all true, Reika."

She nuzzled under his jaw and kissed his throat. "I'm so glad you're mine."

After a long kiss, which required her to touch-up her lipstick and wipe some streaks from his skin as well, he gave her the box of chocolates in a red satin heart-shaped box and an adorable fuzzy stuffed wolf.

Peering at him with a curious smile, she said, "Wolf?"

"You didn't think I'd give you a bear, did you?"

"I guess not." She laughed, and he grabbed her jacket as headlights flashed in the front window and a horn beeped twice.

He tucked her hand in the crook of his arm and walked her down to Jason's SUV and opened the back door for Reika. When Jason's daughter Lyric was born last summer, he had ditched his pickup truck in favor of a more family-friendly vehicle. Bo relished the opportunity to upgrade his own truck, too.

Candles and soft music greeted them as they walked into the restaurant. He was glad to see that they'd been able to replace the front doors so quickly and repair the damage. He had worried that it would set back the special opening, but the whole pack came together to make sure it would happen.

Luka, one of the wolves living with Reika's brother, Ben, ushered them to a table near the center of the room. Bo held out Reika's chair and Jason held out Cades', and when they were all seated, Luka handed Jason and Bo the wine lists and waited patiently for their orders.

There was a little discussion about what to drink, and in the end, they all forewent the wine and chose sweet tea. Jason offered to remain sober while the rest drank, but Bo happened to want to be entirely sober himself. In fact, since Reika had come into his life, he hadn't had a drop of beer or any kind of alcohol. Before, he had used it to numb himself to his pain and misery. But Reika had changed all of that for him, without him even realizing it. He certainly didn't miss the hangovers, that was for sure.

Reika was his drug of choice now. He was completely addicted to her smile, the mischievous glint in her eyes when she was teasing him, the seductive way she walked when she was turned on.

Their drinks and the first course arrived, a small plate of scallops done three ways.

Cades and Reika began to talk about the February full moon and the get together that their pack always enjoyed before the hunt. When Cades explained how a group of she-wolves always followed her back to the house after she stood with Jason as his mate and female alpha, Reika glanced at him, her brow drawn in confusion.

Jason stepped in. "Only unmated females guard Cades, although my mother does from time to time as well. You and Bo are mates.

You need to hunt together and share this unique aspect of your lives together."

"How do I get into the ranking system?" Reika asked.

Cades answered, "Normally, new females fight in wolf form. But Jas and I actually discussed this at length, along with the elders and the other highly ranked wolves, including your mate." Cades' shifted a side glance to Bo who just smiled. She continued, "We would like to offer you the position of *lykar*, which means 'healer.' Like Teller, who is our pack tracker, your position is still under me and Jason as your alphas, and you are required to defend those under you if the need arises, but you are not up for rank fights and are considered a treasured, highly ranked pack member. How do you feel about that?"

Bo looked at Reika's wide eyes and partially opened mouth and grinned. She was actually speechless.

After a few seconds, she cleared her throat and said, "It would be my honor."

Jason nodded and slipped his arm around Cades. "When you and Bo declare each other as mates and we induct you into the pack, we'll specify your title and rank as well. Bo said his aunt would like to work with you from time to time. I'll be sure to let our pack know they can see you through her, if they have a problem."

She nodded and laced her fingers through Bo's hand and squeezed. "If it's an emergency, they can call me now that I have a new cell."

Bo squeezed her hand back. "Just remember our deal."

"Right." She chuckled and said, "No licking without you there."

"You make it sound so dirty," he laughed, releasing her hand to pull her close and kiss her temple.

The rest of the meal passed quickly. The next course was a frilly salad with roasted pears. And then an amazing, thick filet mignon with a mile-high pile of mashed potatoes and roasted asparagus. For dessert, each couple shared a delicious chocolate soufflé.

Glancing around the restaurant as he settled back in his chair with Reika leaning against him, he smiled at the people he considered family. Mated pairs of all ages from their pack filled the restaurant and shared not only the holiday, but they also celebrated the opening of the restaurant that as far as he was concerned, was an unqualified success.

Karly stopped by after the dessert dishes were cleared and they were sharing a cup of coffee before heading home, and Reika's brother joined her. Ben beamed with pride when everyone complimented the food, and Karly heaped praise on her new sous chef.

That night, when he and Reika were alone in his house and passion swirled between them, he dropped down to one knee and pulled a ring box from his pocket. He'd hidden it inside his coat pocket, and snagged it from the depths when he hung it up.

"Reika," he looked up into her eyes, "I love you from the very bottom of my heart. Whatever heartaches we both shared before, we're together now, and the road we traveled to bring us together was worth the pain and misery to have each other in the end. I will spend the rest of my life making you happy if you'll let me. Marry me, Reika."

"Of course I will!" She smiled as tears spilled over her cheeks. He slipped the solitaire on her finger and stood, catching her in his arms and devouring her in a kiss.

She was so perfect for him. Strong, loving, and fiercely protective of those she cared for. He felt honored to have her in his life.

Picking her up, he carried her into the bedroom where they made love, chasing the darkness from the sky and welcoming the sun with cries of pleasure before they passed out, tangled together.

Chapter Fourteen

Reika shouted as she climaxed for the third time, her body whipped into a frenzy by Bo's talented fingers on her clit as his cock pistoned in and out of her pussy.

"Oh, fuck, yes," Bo groaned, squeezing her hips just shy of painfully hard as his cock spasmed inside her. He caught his weight on his arms as he stretched out over her, nuzzling her neck and licking along the fresh bite marks. Her whole body felt like one throbbing bruise since she'd woken up that morning to her very horny fiancé.

She could recall previous full moons, when the urge to find a hot cock and play with it after a good hunt would course through her body and her mind, but she got tired of the wolves in her home pack only being interested in her for that *one* night and refusing to get attached in any other way. She'd missed out on a lot of dating things because of the blood-debt, but she was getting a new life that was full to the brim with love and passion that she hadn't ever known existed.

She felt Bo's teeth scrape along her collarbone, and she shivered and then smacked his shoulder lightly. "Stop biting me!"

Chuckling, he lifted his head and stared at her with wolf-amber eyes. "I can't help that you taste so good. My wolf is really excited to finally have a mate this full moon."

Her own wolf practically purred right then. "Mine, too."

Bo's parents and older brother, Mack, were in town for the full moon ceremony because she and Bo were joining together as official mates in the pack and he wanted them to share it with them. The night before, she and Bo had taken them to dinner and she got to meet not only his mom and dad and brother, but her new sister-in-law and three nephews. Mack's wife, Colette, was a human, and their three boys were also human. Bo's parents, Dustin and Jessie, were sweet and friendly, and asked Bo and Reika to come visit them in the summer with their pack, in Atlanta.

Bo told her later that his parents had been close to Jason's parents, Tina and Peter. When Peter stepped down because of an injury and Jason took over, Dustin and Jessie chose to leave the Tressel Pack and go back to Jessie's home pack. Bo had stayed behind because he was already out of the house and living on his own and had his friends and a position of high rank in the pack. He visited them a couple times a year.

"So we need to talk about something very serious," she said.

His head lifted quickly and a worried look crossed his face. "What is it?"

"You leaving your wet towels on the bathroom floor. Now that we're engaged and about to become official mates, there are some things I'm going to want to change about you."

His eyes narrowed, and he said, "Oh, I see. And just what else do I need to change?"

She lifted a brow in a dare and said, "You could stop snoring, that would be awesome."

"I do not snore!" he growled.

"Bull. Shit."

He lifted a hand and curled it, meeting her gaze for just a moment before he caught her side with it and started tickling her. She shrieked in laughter and tried to get away from him, but he had her pinned with his body as he tickled her until tears streamed from her eyes and she couldn't catch her breath.

"Who needs to be fixed?" He stopped tickling her but held his hand very close to her side.

"Not you, Bo, never you. You're perfect." She swore, hoping he wouldn't tickle her again.

"Good answer. Still, for good measure …" he started tickling her again, but only for a moment, and then he kissed away her laughter and they made love.

He left her on the bed to go take a shower before they had to leave for the cookout, and she reclined on the bed and sent a few texts to her new pack friends. A towel slung low on his waist was the only thing he wore when he came out of the bathroom, and her body, that had spent most of the day in the throes of crashing orgasms, bloomed to life immediately.

Bo's nostrils flared, and he took in a slow breath that ended in a growl. "We don't have time, but later, baby. Definitely later."

She bit her lower lip at the thought of the pleasures that lay ahead of her that night, and got out of bed to shower. She pushed open the bathroom door to find the floor littered with every towel that had been in the cabinet.

"Bo!" she yelled, trying to hide her amusement at his teasing.

His answer was a chuckle.

Reika took a bite of rare porterhouse from the plate that Bo held with one hand. She was perched on his lap as he sat on a chair in the kitchen of Jason and Cadence's home. The house was bustling with pack members, all congratulating Reika and Ben on joining up. She had seen Ben little over the last two weeks since they had come back to Allen because he was busy with his new job at Lonestar's and his three new buddies – Luka, Drake, and Paul. Reika liked the young men and could tell that Ben fit right in with them. Luka worked as a waiter at the restaurant, and Paul and Drake worked as security guards at the retirement development.

She noticed all four boys were very popular with the single females in the pack, and a bit of sisterly protectiveness flared inside her.

Bo took a bite of steak from the fork she held in front of his mouth, and after he swallowed, he said, "Why do you look like you're going to punch someone?"

She looked away from two girls hanging on Ben's arms and sighed. "I'm just feeling like a big sister right now."

Bo looked towards Ben and then back to her. "I wouldn't worry about him. He's smart and capable, and he's away from home for the first time and probably eager as hell to experience everything life has to offer."

"It's my first time away from home, too," she said as she wiggled her brows. "What else does life with Bo Elliot have to offer me?"

He slipped a hand up to the back of her neck and drew her forward until their mouths were so close she could feel the heat from his breath against her lips. "Anything you want, baby."

She closed the distance to his mouth and kissed him, sliding her tongue into his mouth and tasting the intoxicating mixture of red meat and the man she loved. Her wolf took notice and began pacing her mind, knowing that tonight she'd get to hunt with Bo for the first time. The first of many full moon hunts as mates.

She caught sight of Ben as he extracted himself from the two girls and joined his roommates, and she smiled to herself. Bo was right. Ben was smart, and even if he was a *man*, he was a sweetheart who deserved to have a good time when he'd suffered right along with her for so long. Silently wishing him a happy night, she turned her attention back to her mate, and they finished the steak just as Jason clapped his hands together and called for the wolves to journey to the full moon meeting place.

Bo held her still until the crowd cleared out and it was just the upper ranked members, Karly, Shyne, and Cades. Jason said, "The elders are waiting for us. Let's get this night going."

Bo put Reika on her feet, and they walked out of Jason and Cades' home and into the woods behind their house, where the full moon meeting place was. A firepit in the center of a ring of stones had been filled with wood and burned brightly, lighting up the woods around them.

Reika had seen many mating ceremonies before, but she knew that every pack had their own special customs, and she was excited for what was to come.

Jason called for his high ranked to join him in the circle. Bo squeezed her hand and stepped over the stones, joining Michael,

Linus, Logan, and Cades in the circle. To the side stood Peter and Tina, the former alphas, and the three pack elders, Lon, Dae, and Getty. Each held something in their hands.

The current and retired members of the pack surrounded the circle as Reika stood next to Ben in the chilly night, just outside of the stone circle. The five young wolves who had helped in the restaurant when the lynxes had attacked stood with her and Ben.

Jason called for silence, and it seemed that even the creatures in the woods fell quiet as well.

"When wolves show themselves to be honorable, it is our duty as a pack to recognize and encourage that behavior." Jason motioned for the five young males to step forward and they did. "You showed yourselves to be true pack members, following the orders of those in rank above you and protecting those that were unable to protect themselves. We are grateful for your courage, and in thanks for what you did, I ask you to hunt with the high ranked members tonight."

The young males all grinned as Jason spoke each of their names loudly and the pack applauded while Jason and Cades both shook their hands. The young males, faces glowing with pride, joined the pack away from the circle. The noise from the pack died down again.

"Ben Snow," Jason said with a loud voice. "Do you come to the Tressel Pack willingly tonight, to join with us and share in our joys and in our heartaches? Do you swear to protect those below you, respect those in authority above you, and honor the traditions of our people?"

He answered with a strong voice, "I do."

"Are there any here who can say why this male should not join our ranks? Speak now or remain silent for eternity."

Reika felt the silence around them and felt as if her heart stopped beating until Jason broke it by saying, "State your name."

"Benjamin Tin Snow."

"Welcome, Benjamin. Brother. Packmate."

The crowd repeated the word *welcome*.

Ben stepped back to join his friends and left Reika alone. Jason said, "There are those of our kind who are unique, blessed from the great wolf spirit with powers that are extraordinary. When wolves with special abilities choose to join a pack, their skills are honored and protected by giving them the rank of a treasured member."

He looked at Cades, and she cleared her throat. "Reika is a healing wolf known as an *apex*. Her abilities to heal are incredible, and it is our honor as a pack to have her as a member. To protect her from rank fights so no harm comes to her, she is given the status of *lykar*, known as healer, above all but the alphas."

Cades' gaze settled on Reika, and she said, "State your name, *lykar*."

"Reika Felice Snow."

This time, Jason lifted his head to the sky and unleashed a joyous howl. The pack echoed it, and Reika glanced backwards at Ben with a grin, and he howled, too. Her new pack welcomed her, and both her wolf and her human side were overjoyed.

Peter and Tina handed a strap of leather to Jason, and the three elders stepped forward with three jars.

She and Bo faced each other and took off their jackets, tossing them towards Ben who caught them with a grin. Bo was shirtless, and Reika wore a corset. She smiled as Bo's eyes widened and his nostrils flared.

Love you, he mouthed, and she mouthed the words back.

She and Bo grasped their left hands together between them, and Jason wrapped the one-inch thick strip of leather around Bo's wrist, around their entwined hands, and tucked in the end around her wrist. The mating strap was a symbol of them joining together.

Jason spoke loudly. "We come tonight to join Bo and Reika as truemates. Are there any here who would protest this joining? Speak now or remain silent for all eternity."

Jason looked around the pack slowly, and when he was satisfied, he lifted his voice and began to speak in ancient Greek, what wolves knew as the *Old Tongue*. The elders stepped forward one by one and stood next to Jason, extending an open jar to Jason who put his index finger inside the jar.

When he lifted his finger, it was dark with soot that was the ash of the ancestors of their pack. He brushed a line up the inside of Bo's wrist, following the vein, and then did the same to her, reminding the pack that the ashes were part of the mating ceremony to cause them to remember that the history of their people was their responsibility, to ensure that the traditions and laws of their kind were passed on to their children and future generations.

The second elder joined Jason, who dipped his finger into the next open jar. When he lifted his finger, it was coated with dark liquid. He touched the back of Bo's neck and then the back of Reika's.

It was the blood of a fresh kill, a sacrifice to appease and honor the wolf spirits. Jason thanked the great wolf spirit for allowing the joining to proceed, and he asked for a prosperous hunt.

The third elder came forward, and Bo put his finger in the jar. His oil-coated finger drew an infinity symbol over her heart and then he rested his hand on top of their joined ones. She did the same to him, pressing lightly against his hand when she finished.

Jason rested his hands on top of theirs and said, "The olive tree is sacred to our people as a symbol for eternity. Marked under the full moon, this joining is blessed for all to witness and never forget. This joining is forever and ever, until death parts you and you join again, together, in the great beyond."

Bo pulled her to him with their bound hands and kissed her as the pack cheered and howled. Jason called for everyone to shift and hunt, and all around them, the pack began to strip and shift.

Bo tugged Reika into the woods a ways and stepped behind a tree.

"What are you doing?" She laughed, when he kissed her again and then began to unwind the strap. "We are going to shift, aren't we? I'm looking forward to hunting with my mate for the first time."

He unwound the mating strap and folded it, tucking it into his front pocket. "Of course, baby, but I don't want anyone to see you naked but me."

She cocked her head to the side and smiled at him. "I don't want anyone to see you naked, either."

"'Cause you love me?" He reached for the zipper on the back of the corset.

"'Cause you're mine."

"I am, baby. All yours forever, and you're mine."

They stripped each other quickly, because it was damn cold out, and bowed to the ground and shifted.

Reika loved shifting. The rush of endorphins as her body began to change from her human form to her wolf form was intoxicating. She found herself on all fours and glanced down at her blue-black furry paws and then over to where Bo had shifted into his gray wolf.

He moved to her, pressing his nose against her neck and scenting her. She stood perfectly still while he nuzzled and sniffed all around her, happy growls seeping from his throat. He stopped in front of her, waiting for her to scent him. For wolves, when they first joined with their mates, scenting was a way for their wolf selves to commune together, getting to know the subtle nuances of the scent and sight of their mates.

With a leap, she tackled him, knocking him down to the snow and burying her nose in the thick fur around his neck. He growled lightly, the wolf version of a purr, and his tail flipped a few times impatiently as she scented him. She loved the way he smelled, in both his human and wolf forms. She could find him anywhere, she thought, following his rich, spicy scent. As a wolf, he smelled wild and intoxicating, and she was thrilled once more that they were together and mated.

Hopping away from him, she barked and watched as he leapt to his paws. She darted away, and he followed, catching up to her quickly with his slightly longer legs and they raced through the woods, dodging trees and low shrubs, bounding in and out of the shadows of the bright full moon.

They hunted for hours, until the pull of the full moon eased away from them and they were ready to return to their human forms.

As they padded back towards the full moon meeting place, where their clothes laid waiting, she had never felt such joy. Her first full moon as a free woman, hunting side by side with her powerful, beautiful, amazing mate. At one time, she had felt as if she were cursed to never know passion or love or happiness, but Bo had given her all of that in spades, and she was looking forward to the next chapter in their lives.

As she tugged on her icy pants, she pulled her engagement ring from the front pocket and slipped it on.

"Cold, baby?" Bo found their coats nearby and gave her his, too.

"A little."

"How about a nice, hot bath when we get home?" He swept her up into his arms and kissed her as he began walking back towards where his truck was parked at Jason and Cades' home.

"As long as you keep your icy fingers to yourself." She laughed.

"I'm all about warming you up now, baby." He grinned, and her stomach flipped as she wrapped her arms around his neck.

"I'm so glad you're mine, Bo." She kissed his cheek and rested her head on his shoulder, anxious to get home and warm up in his arms.

"I'm so glad you're mine, too, Reika. Forever."

"Forever."

The End

About the Author

A Midwesterner by birth, R.E. spent much of her childhood rewriting her favorite books to include herself as the main character. Later, she graduated on to writing her own books after "retiring" from her day job as a secretary to become a stay-at-home mom.

When not playing with her kids, wrestling her dogs out the door, or cooking dinner for her family, you'll find her typing furiously and growling obscenities to the characters on the screen.

Her best-selling series The Wolf's Mate, Wiccan-Were-Bear, The Necklace Chronicles, Hyena Heat, Wilde Creek, and Ashland Pride are available now.

Made in the USA
Lexington, KY
01 May 2015